The Good Indian Girl

ANNIE ZAIDI writes poetry, fiction, non-fiction, drama, blog posts, reports and reviews. Her first collection of poems, *Crush*, was published in 2007, and her collection of non-fiction reportage, *Known Turf: Bantering with Bandits and Other True Tales* came out in 2010.

SMRITI RAVINDRA writes fiction and teaches creative writing. She is currently working on her first novel.

The Good Indian Girl

ANNIE ZAIDI AND SMRITI RAVINDRA

zubaan

Zubaan
is an imprint of Kali for Women
128b Shahpur Jat
1st floor
New Delhi 110 049
contact@zubaanbooks.com
www.zubaanbooks.com

First published by Zubaan, 2011
Reprinted, 2012

10 9 8 7 6 5 4 3 2

ISBN: 978 81 89884 81 9
Ebook ISBN: 978-93-81017-41-8

Typeset by: Jojy Philip
Printed at Raj Press, R-3 Inderpuri, New Delhi 110 012

For all Indian girls:

Good, bad, ugly, old, little, perfect, plump,

married, dead.

Contents

Acknowledgements

We would like to thank our families who brought us up as good Indian girls – but not the sort of girls for whom good and bad are black and white – and those who watched us as we learnt to look deeper into the heart of this grey world.

We would like to thank Anita Roy, Urvashi Butalia and the Zubaan team, who took this on so enthusiastically. This book belonged to Zubaan even before the first chapter was written.

Above all, we would like to thank the dozens of women, and men, who loaned us their memories, confided in us and trusted us to treat them kindly when we took their anecdotes and made our fictions out of them.

The Good Indian Girl

Let us begin with a disclaimer. By 'good' one does not mean the opposite of 'bad.'

Good simply means the qualities – and by 'quality' one does not imply any qualitative judgment, one merely refers to the characteristics – that make up what is generally acknowledged as desirable behaviour for a girl on the Indian subcontinent.

Virginity is right up there: top of the list. If you have a reputation as a good Indian girl, virginity is considered a given. If you've lost it, you've lost it. You've also apparently lost the right to be called a 'girl.' Watch some of the films made in the 1980s and there's a good chance you'll come upon a scene where the villain is threatening to rape the heroine (or the hero's sister) and saying something like: 'I am going to make you a woman.'

Ah, virginity! If we could have our way, we'd make sure that even married women stayed virgins. Take a look at the matrimonial columns. The divorcee listings will sometimes include significant phrases like 'Girl returned to home one day after marriage' – a discreet way of suggesting that everything is still intact.

There's a high premium on that bit of membrane down there and many an Indian girl will not give it up so easily. This does not mean she will never give it up, or even that she wants to wait for the *saat pheras,* the *nikahnama,* the vows, the court documents, the whathaveyou. It just means it's not going to be easy.

It means that the average Indian girl would like to think that sex with a lover means more than any *saat-pheras* (*nikah*, church vows, rings, the legal whathaveyou) can possibly mean. She would like to believe it was worth risking the whole *saat-phera* shenanigan, that will make up for the risk of her being a spinster for the rest of her life, or the bankruptcy her dad will gloomily encounter as he coughs up large sums of money and assets to make up for the lack of a membrane. That you (sex with you) are going to make her happy.

We realized pretty early on that being a Good Indian Girl (henceforth referred to as GIG) is about as exciting as being a janitor in a pigsty on a full-time basis. It stinks. GIGdom is tolerable for approximately three days a month.

'Oh!' you're wondering. 'How does a GIG remain a GIG if she practices GIGdom for just three days a month?'

Some philosopher has said (or was it an advertising guru?) that image is everything. You are what people believe you are. You are a GIG if you are seen as one. One doesn't have to *be* good. Deep down in the cesspits of your soul you can be wicked, just as long as no one finds out.

And yes, we anticipated the next question: 'What does a GIG do for the remaining twenty-seven days of the month?'

Honestly, a lot of time is spent mooning over the fact that she is a GIG and how much it sucks. Pitiable as it sounds, this is not such a bad thing.

For one, you get to pity yourself and contemplate the sacrifices you are making in the name of family, culture and nation. You can access a kind of default nationalism through the simple process of not having any fun. Besides, nationalism does good things for one's self-esteem. You can not only believe that you *are* good, and that your elders, brothers, brothers' friends etcetera approve of you, but also that you love your country enough to quash all desires that might upset the cultural apple cart.

Sub-continental 'culture' and tradition mostly nestles in the crowded laps of women – their colourful dresses, their hair, the dupattas on their heads, their sarees draped in a dozen different ways, their cooking from scratch every single day, their making of sweets on festivals, their ability to stay put in iffy marriages, their silence in the face of thwarted desire. Where would Indian culture go, after all, if it wasn't for you, the Good Indian Girl?

That said, let us assure you that the average Indian girl does have some fun. It may not be the same as a bad boy's idea of fun. On the other hand, maybe it is.

Finger Play

Deepti and Preeti would never have endured the trauma of walking down the street had the sun set and the neighbourhood been dark. With the gorge on one side – a deep basin of dark trees, darker flowers, and sounds of who knows what animals and insects – and the trees hissing louder after sundown, like a billion witches, even the braves would be almost running, anxious to be home, safe.

But there was nothing to worry about this morning. The sun was high and the girls were walking towards Hot Breads to try out the new pastry the café had advertised on television.

Yet, Preeti was obviously worried.

"So, you were telling me ... but why were *you* drying the clothes?" Deepti asked. "Where was Soni?"

Soni was the maidservant at Preeti's house and of course, it was her job to dry out the clothes, not Preeti's.

"They needed her in the kitchen," Preeti said.

Deepti nodded. That was understandable.

"Then?"

"Then? Then I was on the terrace spreading out the clothes and I saw these guys, sitting behind our compound, near that disgusting sewer. And I was like, 'Eww, that's disgusting!' There were like, six of them. It wasn't like I was really looking at them or anything, or even really thinking about them but they were right there, within the range of my vision. I guess I was kind of blank in the head, you know? Pretty mad at everyone. Ever since we moved into this neighborhood, it's like, don't do this, don't do that. It's boring."

"What about the guys?" Deepti asked.

"So, they were there and I happened to be watching them, just like that. Without really meaning to, you know. Just to have something to do while hanging out the clothes. Then, these guys started going into the bushes. And I was like, 'Ewww! Why don't you just pee into the sewer?' I mean what's the point of going into bushes if there is a river of pee flowing right in front of you? But then! I noticed they weren't going into the bushes to pee. They were plucking leaves. I was still watching them, just casually, without meaning to or anything. The boys plucked leaves, crushed the leaves upon their palms and ate them, like tobacco. You know how it is? I figured, I could see them from the terrace, but they could not see me."

"Sure they couldn't. Not clearly at least."

"Yup, exactly my point. Besides, they were just a bunch of goofers and what did I care if they saw me or not?"

"Must be doing drugs."

"Yup, I asked Praveen later and he said there is marijuana growing by the sewer. Ewww! Isn't it disgusting to be eating anything by the sewer? I wouldn't eat any stuff from there, not for a million bucks."

"Yeah."

The girls were quiet for a while after that, sucking on their bits of tart candy. The warm sun had pulled out barefoot children and dogs with matted hair. The mothers basked in the sun. The women oiled each another's hair. The bitches scratched.

"All this is nothing," Deepti said. "Why are you so worried?"

"They were a bunch of cheapsters, that's why. So, I am watching and thinking that they can't see me. Then someone starts pointing at me and I think, 'Oh, what does it matter? I must look so small from so far'. So I keep spreading out the clothes. And you cannot even imagine what happened next. This one guy – his hair was all long and all – this guy, he pulls something out of his pocket and starts looking through it. I think it was a pair of binoculars."

"Oh!"

"Yup! These guys must be watching women through windows, movie style."

"Yuck!" said Deepti.

"I know. It's totally ewww, isn't it? Then the binoculars were passed around and for once, I was so embarrassed about being in shorts. Thank god my shirt was a loose one."

"Well," said Deepti, looking her up and down, giggling. "You have as fine a pair of boobs as you have legs."

"Shut up. It was creepy, the whole binocular business. Whoever heard of binoculars being so readily available?"

Deepti covered her mouth with her hands and giggled louder.

"You don't understand," said Preeti. "They were so irritating that I finally stuck my tongue out at them."

"You stuck your tongue out at them!"

"Yes. Then I gave them the finger."

"You gave them the finger!"

"Shut up. Now, every morning, when I go out, I have to walk past them, sitting on the Dimple Video Store stairway. I don't know what to do. I don't want to mess with these people. Every time I pass by, they stick their tongues out and call me their morning glory. I hate it. And I hate that I was wearing shorts that morning."

"You know," said Deepti, "I am curious about the boys. Do you think they will be by the store right now?"

"Maybe. Stop laughing Deepti. I don't want to get into trouble with these guys. This neighborhood scares me. Everything out here feels totally temporary, you know what I mean? I mean, even the shops seem to have invisible wheels under them, as if they will suddenly roll away one night and that will be that. Even the houses have that temporary look. I mean, our house looks like a palace or something just because our roof is not made of tin. You know what I mean?"

"It's an all right place. Anyways, if you don't like it here you can always come live with me. Our neighborhood isn't that bad. Hey! Are those the boys?"

And very suddenly, as if it had indeed sprouted wheels and rolled up, Dimple Video Store was right there. And so were the boys, sitting on the staircase: slumped, sprawled, taking up almost half the narrow street.

"They are a bunch of hippies," said Deepti, happy with what she saw. "Is that guy with the guitar your binocular-man? He is kind of cute."

"Shut up."

Preeti gave Deepti a little shove and they began to walk faster. Preeti looked down and counted potholes. Deepti took small glances and was increasingly convinced that the guitar boy was the handsomest boy she had ever seen. He looked like Hritik Roshan.

Hritik Roshan stopped strumming his guitar and instead began to strum the girls with his eyes. The rest of the troupe had on grins as long as the river Nile.

"Hey! Morning Glory," Hritik Roshan called out, and whistled. "Where to?"

"Stupid," murmured Preeti under her breath.

"To your grave," Deepti called out.

Preeti giggled. "Stop it," she said.

"My grave is right here, by my side," Hritik Roshan patted the cement.

"Then what are you doing outside in broad daylight, Mister Dracula?" Deepti asked.

"I like warm blood. It gets too cold at night," said Hritik Roshan.

"Why? What happened to your blood? The wind dried it out?"

Hritik Roshan smiled. "What is *your* name, Morning Glory?" he asked.

"My first name is 'Your' and my last name is 'Sister'. Your Sister," Deepti threw back.

"Awww. That's a sad name. Will no one marry you, or even be your boyfriend?"

"Asshole."

"What? What was that?"

Preeti tugged at Deepti's hand. "Come on, let's go."

The boys laughed.

Hritik Roshan said, "This 'Your Sister' is one hot chilly."

"Yes she is," said Preeti, beginning to get angry. "And you don't want her on your case, believe me."

The boys, in a fantastic chorus, sang out, "Oh yes, we do!"

Preeti and Deepti looked at one another, looked at the boys, and as one, they gave the boys the finger. Then they stuck out their tongues.

The boys bowed and returned the gesture. They showed the girls the finger and they stuck out their tongues.

The girls took it a step further. They brought down their right hand edgeways, like it was an axe, and made a gesture that seemed to cleave the middle finger on the left hand into two. Then they stood there, cocky, hands on hips.

The boys groaned. They held out their middle finger, as though broken, and went into dramatics. The boys would have collapsed had Hritik Roshan not made the gallant effort and recovered from the obvious pain of castration and mutilation.

He plucked a bottle of glue from the wind. Carefully and diligently he poured out a blob from the bottle upon his palm. He then lovingly put back the two pieces the girls had axed. Once the two pieces became one again he held aloft his middle finger, like a proud flag-pole, and sang the national anthem. Subsequently, he offered the flag-pole to the girls.

The girls were not deterred. They conjured up a massive pair of scissors and carved up the flag-pole into a veritable pattern.

With every snip the boys groaned louder. The pain was unbearable. And once again the boys would have collapsed but they followed Hritik Roshan and settled down with needles and threads. Painstakingly, they sewed back the pieces. Those who did not know how to sew took longer and did a rather sorry job, but all in all, the patch-work was functional. Quality aside, the surgical job was done on the shredded middle finger. Duly, it was presented to the girls.

The girls had had enough. They held the offering with both their hands and yanked. They reached forward, grasped, and pulled. They wrenched and tugged and grunted with effort till the finger came off its very base and struggled between the girls' fingers like a lizard's tail. "Hunh," said the girls and swinging their arms chucked the baseless finger into the deep, dark gorge.

The trees realigned themselves to forever sabotage the organ and animals sprinted up to chew on it. But one of the boys, bless him, leaped into the air and like a fielder on the cricket field caught the finger before it even touched the ground. "Out!" he cried in jubilance, and passed it back to the girls.

"No way," cried the girls. They took the pathetic finger, bruised and beaten, and using a motor and pestle crushed it to a fine powder. "There," said the girls, and triumphantly sprinkled the powder upon the street like so much ash.

The boys hurried up and scurried about like rats. The wind came up to scatter the powder and the boys doubled their efforts. They swept frantically, going from one end to the other, running on their toes, moving their hands faster than they ever had. It took forever but atom by atom, millimeter by millimeter, they spotted every particle and gathered them into a dusty heap. By the end of the exercise they were panting and sweating and looking particularly mournful. They did not know what to do with the little heap before them.

"How could you!" cried poor Hritik Roshan. "You have ruined our lives. And by extension, yours too."

"Oh, we will be just fine, thank you very much," Deepti said.

"Come on, give us at least a little bit of your candies. Please."

Preeti tore a piece off her tart strip of candy and gave it to Hritik Roshan.

"What about us?" The other boys asked.

"Go buy some," Preeti made a face at them and stuck out her tongue. The boys stuck theirs out at her.

"So," said Preeti, "why do you carry the binoculars?"

"They're not mine. My brother got them from America."

"And you use them to watch women?"

"You wish!" Hritik Roshan laughed. "I only had them that one day."

"Hmmm, okay, good. Now we are getting late. We are going."

"Where are you off to?"

"We told you," Deepti said. "To your grave."

"And I told you it is right here."

But the girls had started to walk away. They swished their hips and smiled.

"My name is Vikas," Hritik Roshan said.

"Good."

"What's yours?"

"Your Sister," the girls said. And giggled.

Our mothers sometimes say that the younger generation is not capable of imagining the stunts they had pulled off – climbing guava trees, eating raw mangoes, chasing around with sticks. They don't say 'chasing boys' but we imagine that it must have been boys. Where is the 'stunt' factor if a girl only chases other girls in mango orchards?

Some of those stories, we tend to roll our eyes at. Guava trees? Raw mangoes? Little girls chasing little boys armed with sticks? It was a scene out of some film with a rustic setting. Surely, they imagined all that!

And yet, we have no difficulty believing that our mothers had a naughty past, even if it was an imaginary one. There had to be something in their lives that brightens up fading eyes and makes them laugh quietly at untold, guilty secrets.

Strangers

Every second and fourth Saturday, Vandana and Kirti discussed boyfriends. Boyfriends were difficult to come by unless you looked and dressed a certain way and chances of dressing and looking that certain way was near impossible within Marshall's strict code. The nuns who ran the hostel were against anything short, tight or sleeveless. "Sleep decently dressed," they said, "so if you were to die in your sleep, you would still die respectfully."

So on the second and fourth Saturdays of every month, Vandana and Kirti discussed boyfriends and clothes. Just where could they go to exchange their salwaar kameez for the outlandish, translucent lizard-print pyjamas they had bought in Pushkar? Dilemma, dilemma!

Finally, after much trial and error, Tandoor Non Vegetarian Restaurant and Bakery was settled upon. It was in Tandoor's not-too-clean restroom that Vandana, Kirti, Sophia, and Divya removed their conservative kameezes and came out transformed from nun-run-hostel girls to bold, hippy phenomena in floral scarves, sleeveless vests, and reptile pants. The girls were now as ready and hot as that Sunday morning.

The morning was hot and the road shimmered with mirages and fumes. The girls stood on the sandy sidewalk and waited for the appropriate vehicle. Not any vehicle would do. The vehicle had to be a car. No motorcycles or scooters. No more than two boys in the vehicle. Two was already a somewhat precarious number since the girls were only four. A single boy amidst four girls would have been easier to handle, but the girls were ready for two males if it came to that, since they carried pepper powder in their bags. A few cars had to be ignored because of the number of boys seated within, and others because the boys were not good-looking enough. Looks were a criteria too.

But the morning was too warm for infinite waiting so the girls eventually settled upon the blue Maruti with the two boys in the front. The car trembled up from the dip of the road and the girls thrust their breasts out under their flimsy shirts and waved, the paraphernalia of bands, bangles and chains jingling upon their wrists. The vehicle screeched to a halt.

"Hey," said the girls, smiling, tilting their heads.

"Hot day, huh?" The driver rolled his window down. There was on his lip a tiny mole.

"Very," said the girls.

"Want a ride?"

And so it began. The Maruti slid like a drop of rain upon the fuming, vacant, almost empty road. It slid past stray dogs and overworked camels and the girls felt the recklessness of the day. They wondered how it would end. What exactly would happen to this pulsating Sunday afternoon?

The girls lied when the boys asked them their names. The boys let the girls know that they knew they were being lied to but were playing along. The girls played innocent and felt very sexy. The boys played sexy and felt curiously innocent, like children upon a stage.

The girls slipped and the boys slipped and before the end of the hour the two boys, Rahul Liker and Manish Shukla, knew the girls' names: Vandy, Kriti, Soph and Div. Just slipping up thus, mistakenly revealing their real names, left them giddy with excitement. They squealed and giggled at their mistakes. They hit the boys on their arms and were wonderfully abusive. The boys laughed and said “Oops” when the tyres bounced in and out of potholes. The girls called Rahul, “Hey, Liker!” and they winked, as though at a secret. They teased and called Manish ‘Bobby Deol.’ Once, Vandana touched his cheeks and said, “Oh, these dimples!” and Manish felt warm all over his body. It was a heady, heady day.

The boys touched the girls’ scarves and asked which shop sold such accessories. The girls poked the boys through their shirts and questioned them about their goals in life. They looked out the window and discussed shopping options in this little town with the convent and the lake. They wondered if they should drive towards the lake and take a boat ride. They slapped one another on the biceps. They thought this sly sun, this craftiness, this bizarre accident would go on forever, even after sunset, when the convent would beckon to the girls and the boys would be pulled back into their houses by their parents.

Once the boys asked, “Will you meet us again next Sunday?” and the girls said, “Un-huh” and nobody could tell what that meant, not even the girls.

They were a little in love and wondered if this was what everyone talked about, this racing bloodstream, this inability to stop talking, this buzzing car upon a silent road. So they asked a few personal questions. “What do your parents do? What school do you go to?” They meant really to ask, “Are you also a little in love?” but it was too early for that.

Rahul’s father had a shop. Manish’s father had a shop too, except that he imported from Japan, so the girls asked Manish more questions. Had he ever been to Japan? No. But he would definitely get there soon, etcetera.

They did not feel the need to eat lunch. Lunch was boring – sitting at a table and talking to waiters. No. Instead, they craved chaat and chowmein and paper plates with hot bun tikkis steaming on them. A cup of chai to end with. The girls in their lizard pants felt so Indian, so modest, and the boys, in their slippers and with their sleepy eyes thought they would die of joy. So lunch was decided against and the car continued to cruise across town. They went to the lake and sat with their legs in the water. The pedal boats were too intimate for a first Sunday out. Imagine if one of the girls should fall and if one of the boys should jump in to save her and if both should get wet! Imagine! So they did not buy a ticket for pedal boats and satisfied themselves with talking about dreams and hobbies.

Rahul played the guitar. Manish liked to sit outside shops and watch girls. "Though if you asked me to stop, I will never look at another one," he said.

The girls were touched.

It was not so warm in the evening and now when they returned to their cars they rolled the windows down and let the wind ruffle their hair and scarves. They talked loudly to outdo the whistling wind and to overcome the regret of having to return. The road, neat and undisturbed under the afternoon sun, was tousled with people and vehicles. It was a pleasant evening. They decided to go for the chaat they had been craving and drove to mall road where carts and *tokaries* sold spicy snacks and ripe fruit. Men, women, children stood around eating *kachori* and *mirchi wada*. The girls looked out of the window and pointed at the last cart. "That is where the best chaat is sold," they said.

As they inched towards the best chaat cart, Divya spotted Sister Francie amidst the carts, sampling the fruits. Sister Francie looked slim and fashionable in her white tunic and wimple. Other women with their flower-print kurtas and modern jewellery seemed outdated in contrast.

And it was then that the fear rose. If Sister Francie saw the girls, dressed as they were, in a car with boys... who knew what Sister Francie would say? What report would she carry back to the school? What would the Principal demand to know?

Divya nudged Sophia and pointed at Sister's lackadaisical form moving from cart to cart. "We have to get out of here," she said. Sophia froze. The horror of being expelled from the convent, or even being momentarily suspended, became real and terrifying. There would be notes sent to parents. There would be tales told among relatives. There would be permanent damage on character certificates. It would become impossible to get admission in good colleges. The nuns would definitely mention lizard-print pyjamas and shirts without sleeves. Perhaps some of the girls in the hostel would call them sluts.

At the last cart, the girls asked to be dropped off. The car came to a grudging stop. Burdened with the implications of the abrupt silence, Kirti said, "Hey, we are not really from Bhutan, okay? We are from here only."

The boys nodded. Kirti had broken the masquerade and they were all sad. The lies – outrageous and ridiculously simple – had felt so silly and sweet.

"All righty then," said the girls.

They stepped out of the car, one by one. The boys stepped out too. How awful farewells are!

There was a crowd in front of the stall – it was a popular place, the best pani-puri in town. The boys were awkward. Could they expect more? Would there be a meeting next week? Could they shake hands? Could they expect hugs?

The girls were already moving away, their smiles fading as they mingled with the crowd. The boys were apprehensive. This could not be the end of it all, could it?

"Could we pick you up next Sunday?" Rahul asked, breathless.

The girls turned around as one, smart in their solidarity. In a chorus they said, "Excuse me?"

"Could we meet again next Sunday?" Rahul repeated, embarrassed at having to ask again.

"Do we know you?" The girls frowned. They looked around. "Are you talking to us?"

"Very funny," said Rahul.

The girls shrugged and shook their heads – they had no clue who these boys were.

"Hey, come on!" Rahul said, laughing nervously. "Enough of this joke, okay?"

"Look, please don't pester us. Either you have us confused with someone else, or you are trying to act smart."

"Neither," said Manish. "You girls are sick."

But the girls started to move away.

"We will get you," Manish said, his voice hard.

"Try touching us," Vandana said, "and the crowd will beat you senseless."

So the boys stopped. It was true. The crowd would beat them senseless.

Good girls with their sweet names.

Preeti – name of the beloved. Deepti – a lit lamp of a name. Vandana, Sophia, Divya, Kirti – names that are respectable embodiments of what parents and grandparents want a GIG to be as an adult. The elders certainly hope that their baby girls will grow up like a prayer, like a wise creature aglow with light, one whose fame spreads far and wide.

But how far, how wide? That's a catch no GIG knows how to elude. Who may be familiar with her, who may call her, what conclusions might be drawn from the fact that a stranger knows something about her – even just her name?

It was hard to get any straight answers. We asked ourselves: do we care if a random stranger (male) digs up some information about us, like our name or address? Well, we think, not really. But what if a stranger assumes that knowing our names was the same as knowing us? Would it still not matter? More importantly, should it not matter?

Perhaps, the right person to answer these questions would be a good Indian boy. We found one and asked him for an answer, but all he gave us were his memories.

Name Games

Hi. My name is Angad.

About GIGs, what do I say? I can only say that I've had really bad luck with them.

The first time I started thinking about 'good' girls was in high school in that small hill town where I grew up.

I had just cleared my tenth boards. I never took my exam results personally but it was clear the examiners hadn't taken a shine to me. My father was not thrilled to discover that I was in the bottom third of my class. The senior secondary exams decided the course of one's life and, at this rate, my life seemed headed straight into the gutter stream of the humanities. So, during the summer vacation, my father made me join coaching classes for physics, chemistry and maths. Four hours a day, every day.

My mother took pity on me and had me join violin classes in the evenings. "To help him relax and improve concentration," she told my father.

The tuition centre and violin classes were both sexual deserts. The violin teacher took two batches every evening – 4pm to 5.30pm for girls; 6.30pm to 8pm for boys. There was a whole hour between the two batches so that there was no question of any overlap. If a boy stayed on that street long enough to see any girls, you could safely assume he was hanging around waiting to see girls. This would be noticed by the teacher, and your parents were sure to be called. So none of the boys hung around hoping to meet girls.

But fate seemed to have singled me out for reprieve. Reeta appeared in town.

It was the day my bicycle broke down. To save the rickshaw fare, I decided to walk to my violin class. I saw a girl walking towards me, a violin case in her hand. She noticed the violin I was carrying and gave me a tiny smile. I returned her smile.

I didn't take my bicycle to the repair shop the next day. I walked again. Once again, I met her walking back. She smiled again.

Three days of this and my father, annoyed at my laziness and time-wasting habits, got my bicycle repaired. I had no excuse to set out earlier. I had to cycle to class and didn't see the mystery girl for a week. Then one afternoon, the bicycle tyre ran out of air. I was wheeling my bike along and there she was. This time, I gathered courage.

"Hi."

It was a vague, non-committal smile. Or so I thought. What did I have to lose? The girl was an outsider. Maybe her family was staying just for the summer.

"My name's Angad," I said.

"Reeta," she said.

I couldn't think of anything else to say. I just stood there staring at the wheels of the bicycle. I don't think I had even looked properly at her face and had no idea whether I found her attractive or not.

She broke the silence, "So, you don't come every day?"

"I do. But it takes only fifteen minutes on a cycle. Today I am early."

No more explanation was needed. She nodded.

"My name is Reeta," she repeated. Then we walked away in opposite directions.

My bicycle tyre was pumped up that day. I didn't dare set out early with my father watching my 'time-wasting ways'. I didn't see her for weeks. Then one day, I saw her in the market.

It was somebody's birthday and all the tuition centre boys had taken permission from their fathers to go out. We were in an ice-cream parlour when I spotted Reeta with two other girls.

I didn't say anything but one of the other boys promptly leaned across the table. He whispered, "See that girl? The one in the green suit? I know her. Her name is Reeta."

Another boy laughed. He didn't bother to whisper. "So what? Everybody knows that."

"Really?"

"Oh yes," he sniggered. "Everyone in this town knows Reeta. Even the paan-walas and rickshaw-walas. She talks to anyone, tells them her name."

I concentrated on my ice-cream. Then one of the boys threw out a challenge.

"So let's see if you know her. Call her. Call out to her. We'll see how much you know her."

The boy who had spoken first began to snigger. He kept sniggering as he licked his ice-cream spoon. Just as Reeta was about to leave the parlour with her friends, he called out.

"Reeta! Hello!"

Reeta swung around, and began scanning faces at our table. The other boys began to laugh. Nobody said a word. They just laughed. Reeta's eyes were on my face. Her friends tugged at her hands and the girls left.

I wanted to say something in that ice-cream parlour. I wanted to say that maybe the whole world knew her name – and it was easy to know anyone's name – but they didn't really know *her*. How can anyone really know anyone else? I talked to these boys every day; we spent four hours a day together. But I didn't know them and they didn't know me. They didn't know their own mothers. I wanted to tell those boys that knowing a girl, really knowing her, was an accomplishment none of us would ever have. We were thick-headed and they were complex. We were impatient and territorial, insensitive louts. Just look at us! Assuming we could grab some piece of a person when all we had access to was the sound of her name! I wanted to tell the boys they were all dolts and girls were far out of their reach. We were pitiful. I wanted to say all this. But I didn't.

I finished my ice-cream and we all pooled our pocket money to pay the bill.

I think of that day even now and I feel I should have said something. I should have spoken to Reeta, or tried to meet her and apologize somehow. But I just didn't know how. We didn't talk to each other, girls and boys, in that small town. Maybe you have to understand that place, that kind of school to understand why I was so helpless.

Ours was a co-ed school but until high school, we only noticed the girls during annual day celebrations, when they were dressed up in saris. We played in separate parts of the playground. Inside classrooms, the girls sat up front in the first three or four rows, and the boys took up the rest of the seats, further away from the blackboard. Those boys who sat just behind the girls were either the academically inclined ones, or short-sighted. Those who were keenest on getting female attention sat right at the back and they occasionally let out soft, hollow-sounding whistles that echoed too loud in the whitewashed classroom.

There were only three boys who sat right next to girls in the fourth row, because there weren't enough girls to fill that row of desks. One of these boys was me.

It was the science section; we were in Standard XI and life was one long blur of books. But one small welcome note of relief came in the form of a teacher from Goa. She taught the nursery classes but she sometimes filled the free periods for senior classes. Miss encouraged us to make scrapbooks instead of just making us open our notebooks and mug up whatever needed to be mugged. She was a great believer in extra-curricular activities for 'overall, broad-based, personality development'.

I made a cricket scrapbook. I pasted in pictures of all the Indian cricket captains since 1947, with little notes underneath, citing world records and landmark victories. There was this girl, Mehek, whose desk was in the fourth row. I knew her name only because she answered to the name at roll call. We never spoke, though.

Mehek made a scrapbook on Bollywood film stars. This should have been a popular theme because photos and gossip were so easy to find. But most students were afraid to choose films because it would reflect badly on their choices in life. Cricket, being a sport, had some sort of respectability attached. After all, the best colleges had sports quotas. Ever heard of a 'film star quota' in any university?

Mehek was brave to have picked her theme. Somebody was sure to disapprove of the scrapbook, probably her own parents. I thought of her sitting at home, sifting through film magazines, cutting out photos, gathering trivia. It must have taken a certain amount of courage to waste time so outrageously, so exquisitely uncaring of what anyone might think or say.

One day, I reached school fifteen minutes early. Mehek was already in class, working on her scrapbook. I found myself asking, "Can I see?"

She looked up and silently pushed the book towards me. I started turning the pages.

There was Amla first, then Anita Raj, Babita, Dimple Kapadia, Geeta Dutt and so onwards to Mamta Kulkarni – just looking at that photo was enough to make the blood rush to my face – followed by Meenakshi Sheshadri and so onwards to Sonam in really short denim shorts, bending at the waist, leaning towards the camera. It was all very sexy. After Sonam, three whole pages were devoted entirely to Sridevi.

The last photo of Sridevi was one in which she was wrapped in a towel, a little finger caught saucily between her teeth. I suppose I must have looked at that photo for a long time. When I looked up, I saw Mehek watching me.

She looked at the page I was on, then she looked at me again, and suddenly she started blushing furiously. I felt strange, as if I had done something inappropriate. So I closed the book and went to sit at my own desk.

Later that day, our Goan teacher asked how we were faring with our scrapbook projects. We duly trooped up to her desk with our books, peeked into others' books. I was standing near her desk when she began flipping through Mehek's scrapbook.

My chest began to tighten as she flipped the pages, edging closer and closer to the towel-only photo of Sridevi. I was afraid but I still don't understand why – afraid for Mehek? For Miss? For what Miss might think about us collectively?

Meanwhile, Madhuri gave way to Meenakshi, Nargis to Padmini, Rati to Sandhya to Sonam to Sridevi. My heart beat faster but when I glanced down, the towel-only photo wasn't there. From a photo of Sridevi in a snow-white pantsuit reclining on a snow-white bed, the book skipped straight to a black and white photo of Tanuja in black pants and grey pearls.

Even Miss seemed to have noticed that something was amiss. I watched her frown and flip back to Sridevi. She took the page between her thumb and forefinger and rubbed the edges. The corner of the page split. Mehek had glued two pages together to hide the towel-only photo.

I shot a glance at Mehek and found that she too was looking at me.

From then onwards, Mehek would glance at me often. I would squirm, feeling the warmth of her gaze spreading on the side of my neck. I kept telling myself that I was imagining it, but each time I turned, she would be looking at me.

I wasn't quite sure what she wanted. She never smiled. She never talked to me. For a few days, I thought she was upset with me, or afraid of me, because I had seen the Sridevi towel-only photo in her book. But soon, other students in class also noticed how often she looked at me.

During lunch break, as the girls huddled around desks in small groups, whispering and giggling over their tiffins, the boys stepped outside. The more sporty ones found a ball to kick around after they finished their snack. Boys like me would sit down on the steps and watch the senior girls strolling past, while pretending to be swotting from our notes.

My 'gang' had five boys in it and all wore glasses. We all read during the long lunch break, sometimes in the library, sometimes on the ledge outside the library. Everyone had found something to talk about: Mehek and her shameless fascination with Angad.

"She likes you," the boys said. They asked me questions about her. Where did she live? What school was she in before this? Did she have sisters? Brothers? I did not know anything and didn't know who to ask. So my gang urged me to find out things about her by following her. It was the tried and tested, time-honoured thing to do. If you liked a girl, you started following her. Of course, if she had an elder brother, or a father who was an army-man or a cop, you had to be discreet. But, the gang pointed out, she was looking at me. It was a green light. It meant 'Go'.

Now, another thing I did not know – and to be fair to my bespectacled gang, I don't think they knew either – was that Bholu liked Mehek too.

Bholu was a year senior and he was in the sporty gang. He played football and cricket and basketball and many other kinds of ball. He sat at the back of the class and claimed to have visited discos in Bombay and he made no secret of the fact that he didn't really like books.

One morning, Mehek and I happened to enter the school gate at the same time. Encouraged by her open interest in me, I called out, "Hi! Mehek, hi! Good morning."

She turned, looked at me sort of coldly, as if I was a stranger who had hailed her on the streets. I blundered on, "Mehek, where do you live?"

She didn't answer but she did glance around nervously. I assumed this was a natural shyness. All girls were supposed to be shy.

"I live near Kaathi Chouraha," and when she still did not say anything, I added, "I don't have any sisters." As if this piece of information might be of particular interest to her.

Clearly, it wasn't. She rushed towards the school entrance and suddenly, she murmured "Sorry" over her shoulder and raced upstairs to the assembly hall.

Later that day, Bholu and his gang came looking for me. They pushed me about, grabbed my collar, undid my tie and slapped the back of my head a few times. In retrospect, they never meant to hurt me. They just wanted me to stay away from 'Bholu's girl'. But it was horribly frightening while it was happening. I still get breathless when I think of it.

I also realized that Mehek's silence had something to do with the fact that Bholu used to follow her about. He would beat up any boy who took an interest in a girl he claimed for himself. I still don't know whether Mehek's interest in me was her way of challenging Bholu, or whether she was simply making a silent plea for help.

I should have steered clear of Bholu. However, my ego was badly bruised. Now the girl actually meant something to me. Not that I was in love with her but I had to save face somehow.

Bholu's gang was a rough lot. It was rumoured they carried knives in their school-bags. I couldn't take them on alone. So I asked my bespectacled gang if they would rough up Bholu the way I had been roughed up. They all just blinked at me through their glasses, eyes widening with alarm, lips curling into shapes of pity and fear.

It was as if they were saying, "Angad's lost it and it should serve as a lesson to us all not to get mixed up with girls."

I was burnt up with anger, consumed with thoughts of revenge. I began to secretly carry a *rampuri* in my school bag, and would finger the blunt outline of the knife for reassurance each time the bell rang for lunch break.

I studied but without concentration. And out of the corner of my eye, I could see that Mehek still stole glances at me. Unexpectedly, the problem was solved after the final exams. Mehek flunked Standard XI.

Now I no longer had to deal with a girl sitting a couple of desks away, making eyes at me. As for Bholu, he flunked too but his family packed him off to a very expensive school in Ooty where the football training facilities were rumoured to be the best in the country.

You know something? It has been ten years since I moved to Delhi but I still have that *rampuri*. I still fantasize about meeting Bholu some day, hopefully in a dark alley.

I imagine him to have grown into a pot-bellied, executive type who wears formal shirts and carries a black briefcase to work. But I recently found out Bholu is still in some university, that he is an up and coming politician. 'Student leader'. Wears white *khaddar* and sandals. I saw a photo in a local newspaper. He does have a bit of a belly though.

Still, I like my fantasy of the plump executive with shiny shoes and a loosened tie around his neck. I see myself bumping into him one dark night. I see myself grab him by the neck, without warning, pushing him up against a wall and slapping his face a few times. I would take out my *rampuri*, holding its blade against his cheek. His eyes would be popping out, his face sweating. And I would say: "So, Mehek is your girl, is she?"

Of course, it's just a childish fantasy. I hope you don't think I mean any of it. I'm a good guy. I don't carry the *rampuri* around. It is lying at home under a mattress.

And no, I certainly don't want Mehek. Or Reeta. The girls don't mean much to me. Their names are part of my childhood, like memories of a battle I did not dare fight. And those are the battles that haunt you for the longest time, right?

Glued-together pages in a filmy scrapbook? Terrified of a favourite actress photographed in a state of suggestive undress?

Seems far out? Can't believe it? Think we're exaggerating? Trust us: it happened! One of these stories was told to us by a friend who grew up to be very poetic, very sexually unapologetic. She had laughed with tears in her eyes as she remembered how innocent, how easily embarrassed small-town schoolgirls can be. It takes so little for them to blush. And it takes absolutely nothing for them to cry.

Cover Judging

Miss Shonali stopped her lesson and looked down the length of the room – a bent head with two neat plaits. The voice that had piped up a moment ago – "Miss! Miss! Anita is crying" – was telling the truth. Anita was indeed crying.

The English (Elective) teacher dropped a piece of chalk on the floor, dusted her hands by briskly rubbing her slender fingers against each other, and walked down to the desk where Anita sat sniffling.

Standard XI B sat motionless, stunned at this sudden descent into saline drama. Eight students knew why the girl was crying and seven of them wanted to throw something heavy at her. They were sure they would never speak to her again; that is, assuming they survived this crisis and were allowed to stay in school.

Miss Shonali was perplexed. She had never been confronted with this sort of situation before – a girl bursting into tears in the middle of a lecture on metaphysical poetry. Usually, there was a lot of laughter whenever they discussed John Donne's work.

Gingerly she patted the girl's head.

"Are you sick, Anita?"

The girl let out one more generous sob.

"Do you have a … a stomachache?"

Seven pairs of eyes glittered and hardened. "Say yes," they collectively willed.

Anita may have felt the prickly beams of light boring into her frame, crawling up her bare forearms, but she didn't look at any of them. She continued to sniffle.

A minute ago, seven pairs of eyes had swung her way, horrified. One of these belonged to Ranjana, whose heart was shrivelling up faster than green chillies left out on a rooftop in an Indian summer. Another heart that was sinking in Titanic style was Amit's, the said organ having only recently recovered from Teena's loss to her new boarding school (co-educational boarding! What sort of mother did she have?).

Miss Shonali was asking now, "Did somebody say something? Anita, speak up."

Ranjana's heart was leapfrogging in her mouth. She wanted to kick her friend's ankles but was afraid to do it right under Miss Shonali's nose. Any second now, the teacher would lean in closer and notice the magazine resting in Anita's lap.

And so the teacher did. She extricated it from under the girl's unresisting hands. A gasp went up from all corners of the classroom. It was the latest copy of *Stardust* and the cover photo was mostly just bare skin.

Several students got to take a good, long look at the cover as their teacher flipped through the magazine. The cover picture was unlike anything they had seen on Indian magazine covers before, though of course, many of the boys had seen everything there was to see thanks to outdated foreign magazines that were to be found at any kabadi-wala's shop at the bottom of the junk-pile, if you went looking.

This particular issue of *Stardust* bore a picture of emerging starlet Mamta Kulkarni (gasp!) bare to the waist. The actress had used her own arms to cover the essentials, but that wasn't all: the zip of her jeans was, rather noticeably, unzipped.

What the rest of the class could not see was the marginalia that had been recently scribbled inside the magazine as it was passed from hand to hand. This note-passing combined with filmy marginalia, this gossipy double-dollop of suspect classroom activity that had been going on for the last few weeks was now resting in the shaking hands of Miss Shonali.

Miss Shonali was popular with the senior classes. The boys especially liked her because she was the only female teacher who minded the boys' staircase. The boys took a flight of stairs up to the classrooms from behind the admin office in the left wing, while the girls took the main set of stairs up from the entrance. There was no written rule about segregating male and female teachers, but most female teachers did staircase duty on the girls' stairs. Miss Shonali was different. She chose to mind the boys' stairs although the male sports coach had pointedly informed her that she was not required to do so.

This little spark of defiance won the students' hearts. A few boys in the senior section had gone up to her to ask for advice on how to approach girls 'for friendship' when they went away to college. She usually laughed at their questions, and freely gave advice. But to carry a magazine with a cover like this, even in liberal little Miss Shonali's book, was a truly naughty thing.

She began reading the notes in the margins, one by one, and her finely shaped eyebrows rose higher and higher and then disappeared into a vile frown. She turned her back on the class and slowly paced between the rows of desks and benches. Up one aisle, down another. Across the room, down the aisle. The magazine was rolled up tight in her hands, and she was smacking her palm with it. That, and the whirring of the fan was the only sound in the classroom. Not one student sniffed, shuffled, whispered or coughed. Some students were not even breathing.

Ranjana certainly was holding her breath. She was hoping that if she held it long enough her face would turn blue and, with any luck, she would collapse. Then, the sympathy factor would override the horror of being declared a slut to the whole school, followed by the inevitable denouement at home. She could, of course, pretend not to have written that note. But Miss Shonali was familiar with the students' handwriting. Damn damn damn Anita!

But Ranjana's constitution proved to be sturdier than she imagined and, instead of turning blue, her face just turned an awkward shade of purple, making her look guilty rather than faint. She tried to remember the exact sequence of words: who'd said what? Monu, if she had it right, had started it all. He'd scribbled a note saying, "Mamta is Mmmmm!"

To this, Amit had appended, "What mums!!" Monu had responded by scribbling, "She must be so hot!!!" Amit had replied, "She looks like she knows it all." He had then turned the page to scribble yet another note: "Do you think Mamta is sexy?" and he passed the magazine on to Manjari, who had replied, "No! She's a slut!" Amit wrote, "Sluts are sexy" and passed the magazine back.

Manjari scribbled, "These boys are yuck. I'm not talking to them" and she passed the magazine on to Ranjana, who wrote, "All boys are yuck." Manjari promptly responded with, "I hope not! Otherwise, what will happen to us afterwards?"

Ranjana had then written, "Do you think all boys are yucky?" and passed the magazine on to a quiet, spectacled boy called Pratham. He had given this due thought, cocking his head this way and that, fumbling with a ballpoint. "Yes. They are on single track. But SOME are decent also." 'Some' was heavily underlined.

Tushita who sat next to him and read every single note passed on to or through Pratham, wanted to butt into the conversation. So she too scribbled a note, "I am mostly afraid of boys. Only Pratham is very sweet." She passed the magazine on through Pavitra, who scribbled, "I'm not afraid of boys. But I will be very afraid one day. The day I am getting married."

Pavitra passed the magazine back to Ranjana, who added her own note, "I'm not afraid of getting married, but I am very afraid of the wedding night." And then she caught Anita's eye just as she was about to pass the magazine back to Pavitra.

Anita, who had once been Ranjana's best friend, had been looking on with an accusatory glare at the growing friendship between her ex-best friend and these new people: Amit, Pavitra, Manjari. Out of sheer guilt, Ranjana would include Anita in their conversations and these little classroom games. Which is what she had felt compelled to do once again. In a lame attempt to be inclusive and conciliatory, she passed the magazine to Anita instead of Pavitra.

And Anita started crying.

Ranjana would have kicked herself if she hadn't been so focused on wanting to kick the weeping girl. "This," she thought, "is why Anita can never be my best friend. She cannot even look at a half-naked woman without howling. As if she has something different under her clothes!"

Ranjana had been increasingly exasperated with her friend ever since they passed their tenth boards. Anita was unwilling to discuss hot scenes after watching a film, and it was impossible to get her to talk to the boys about anything except homework. Ranjana should have known that Mamta Kulkarni's unzipped jeans and braless torso would be too much for Anita.

Meanwhile, Miss Shonali had finally stopped pacing and had swung around to glare at the class.

"What," she hissed, "should I do with this?"

The whole class, even those who were not involved, sat with their heads bent.

"Should I," she went on, "take this to the Principal? Should I?"

If Anita hadn't been crying already, she would have burst into tears now. Ranjana made renewed attempts at fainting, and failed yet again.

"The more freedom you children get, the more you abuse it. Is THIS the sort of thing to bring into class? What do you think the Principal will do when he finds out?"

Ranjana shuddered. She didn't know about the Principal, but

she could imagine a few of the things her mother would do. How would she ever explain having written those notes in the margins? How could she even explain having thought about things like weddings nights? For a second, her head spun with the horror of confronting her mother and she almost did collapse, but the second passed and, with a telltale flush on her face, she sat there blinking back tears.

"What," Miss Shonali repeated, "should I do with this? What should be done?"

She paced and paced – up and down, between the rows of desks. And just when it seemed like she was going to step out of the classroom and go fetch the Principal, she came to an abrupt stop.

"Listen! For now, just this one time, I am not going to say anything to the Principal. But if once more, just one more time, I see any notes being passed around, any scribbling, any magazines ..." and she smacked her palm with the rolled up glossy.

Stardust was never seen or mentioned again. Except by Monu. Later, he asked Amit what might have happened to the confiscated magazine.

"You think Miss kept it? Does she read it at home? Maybe she likes looking at such pictures."

Amit, chewing on the end of his tie, offered, "What else? Miss is not all nice-nice. She does staircase duty on the boys' stairs. She doesn't need to, does she? She must be reading such kind of magazines all the time."

Monu kicked a few pebbles around.

"You know, Miss isn't married yet ..." he trailed off.

"But," Amit finished it for him, "she knows everything. Everything."

What's a girl to do if you confront her with lust?

She, who has been taught to grow a mask of stone on her face when she walks outdoors, to pretend she is deaf and blind should a man pay attention to her body?

She, who wears a slip under a school uniform, even in the hottest, most humid climate?

She, whose mother pulled her out of one class and put her in a different one when she was barely seven years old because her best friend was a seven-year-old boy instead of a seven-year-old girl?

She, who read D.H. Lawrence on the sly and liked to look at film magazines splashed with photos of semi-nude actors?

What does she do when confronted with her own lust?

Tiger Balm

Hi! My name is Reeta. To help you understand GIGs, I am going to tell you about this one friend, only I can't tell you her name. Let's just call her Meera.

She is middle-class, well-educated, has a steady boyfriend and lives in a metropolitan city. We used to intern together after our MBA and at one point, we were pretty close. Then I got married and moved to the US and for a while, we lost touch. But now we are back in touch and she treats me like a close confidante.

So, the other day, Meera was upset. She called me up sounding distraught. We went out for a long walk around the colony, like we always do when we need privacy. If you want to know more about GIGs, you should walk around, two steps behind any girls who are walking together and chatting. You should eavesdrop.

Anyway, so I asked her, "What's wrong?"

It turned out that Meera had gone to her boyfriend's place and (this is her version of the story, of course) he started getting all touchy-feely. Which is only natural. I mean, what did she expect? I said as much.

"Did you think he was calling you to his room to feed you *halwa-poori*?"

"He said we would watch DVDs."

Yeah, right! I didn't say it out loud but I knew that she knew that her boyfriend hadn't really meant to just sit cozily to watch films when they were alone together. Even she is not that stupid.

As expected, he did put on a DVD but half-way through, the boyfriend got a bit cuddly. But Deepti promptly pushed him away and told him, "This is not proper."

What? Who 'Deepti'? Oh, did I say Deepti? Sorry, I meant to say Meera. Oh hell! Well, okay, there is no Meera. Okay? It was Deepti I was talking about but please don't tell her that I told you. She's really weird about these things. She's paranoid about anyone finding out about her boyfriend, like it would ruin her reputation or something. I mean, come on! In this day and age! Can you believe it?

But to get back to the story, this poor fellow, Deepti's boyfriend, he looked suitably ashamed of himself when she pushed him away. He began to nod in agreement. "Yes, of course," he said. "This is not proper. I'm sorry."

Deepti said, once again, "We shouldn't be doing this."

He agreed. "No, no, we should not. Of course not."

Deepti said, "We really shouldn't do this before we get married... should we?"

Her boyfriend was getting more and more flustered with each passing second. He said, "No, no, you're right. Absolutely. This can wait. I can wait. I'm sorry."

So they didn't do 'this' and everything went on as before. Quiet coffees and conversation substituted for passion.

I asked Deepti, "So what's the problem? Nothing happened, right?"

She kept quiet for a few seconds, fidgeting and pulling loose threads off the hem of her kurta. Finally, my virtuous little friend burst out saying, "Butbutbut I hadn't really asked him to stop."

"You did," I pointed out. "You pushed him away, and you said you didn't want to do 'this.'"

"Yes, but just because I push him away a little bit, it doesn't mean he should stop," cried Deepti.

That's a GIG for you. Even when she wants it, she doesn't want to feel responsible for it. She wants the pleasure without the guilt. Like Deepti. She wanted to be told that 'this' was okay and that 'this' is what people do when they are in love and there is nothing wrong with making love, especially when you are so committed, that sex is nothing but a beautiful form of self-expression, a sacred thing, in fact.

Even then, there is a good chance that Deepti would have said a flat 'no'. But the truth is that she wanted to feel as if all her inhibitions and protests were swept away, just like it is in all those Mills & Boons she keeps reading. The arrogant, dominating man who can also be very gentle, very skillful, much more in control than she herself is. She wanted the man to decide whether they're going to do it or not.

Anyway, in this case, the man was not being very decisive, much less dominating. And where did that leave my poor, virtuous friend?

A few days after our conversation, Deepti decided to give him some leeway. She went back to his place, and this time, it was she who suggested that they watch some DVDs. Her poor boyfriend was confounded. He didn't know how to interpret this but he decided to play it safe. He obediently put on a DVD and this time, he didn't get touchy-feely.

Deepti could not concentrate on the movie at all. She fidgeted. She drank water. She reclined on the floor. She shut her eyes.

Her boyfriend watched, alarmed, not knowing what to make of it all. After half an hour, Deepti declared that she had a bad headache and she did not want to watch any DVDs. So her boyfriend jumped up at once and asked if she wanted a Disprin.

She said, "No, it's a regular migraine. Disprin doesn't help. Only Tiger balm will help now."

So the boyfriend quickly got her some Tiger balm. Meanwhile, Deepti had stretched out on his bed. Very, very timidly, he asked, "Should I rub in the balm?"

She just kept her eyes shut, and deigned to let a 'hmm' escape her throat, as if she was doing him a favour.

Poor Mister Boyfriend began to rub Tiger balm on her temples and then he gave her a head massage while he was at it. And then?

Well, in Deepti's words: "Then what? Nothing happened. Cheapo!"

But I am not at all convinced that 'nothing happened'. Because she no longer tells me what her boyfriend did *not* do to her. Besides, she seems to have finally found a good cure for her headaches. I don't hear any more stories about Tiger balm these days.

Boyfriends. A tricky, touchy subject with many Indian girls. You want one, but you don't really want to be seen as having one. And even if you do, you definitely don't want to be seen as someone who gets sexually intimate with this boyfriend.

It isn't about being polite or discreet, the way many married couples are – not a hint of lustful encounters under the blankets the moment they step inside the bedroom. Looking at these couples, one is tempted to believe that every other child on the subcontinent came from the Immaculate Conception school of manufacturing.

Most GIGs grow up valuing notions like love, belonging, and holy matrimony. But they prefer to think of love as a non-platonic relationship, not a sexual affair. They prefer that their boyfriends think of them as beautiful, physically desirable creatures, but they don't necessarily want their boyfriends to think that they have aggressive physical needs. They want to be seen as shy, confused girls. Like a blushing bride sitting on a flower-bedecked bed, waiting for the man of her life to lift her face to his own and demand that she love him.

It is possible, of course, that Reeta's analysis is all wrong. We decided to go back and ask the lady in question – are GIGs truly reluctant to take responsibility for their bodies, are they ashamed of their own lust? More importantly, is Tiger balm all that it is cut out to be?

Stop Press

What? Wait! No! That Reeta is such a liar!!! I swear to god, everything she said actually happened in the reverse.

Oh, alright. We'll do this your way. Hi! My name is Deepti. Did you write it down? Did you write down everything Reeta said? Okay, then you have to write down what I am saying too.

Yes, I used to be friends with Reeta. Hell, yes, *used to be*! Past tense. I'm done with that smutty woman.

The truth is that Reeta – married and mother of one, please note – was trying to cootchiecoo with some new fellow. But she was getting nothing out of him and she couldn't take the blow to her ego. She wanted to talk about it, I guess, so she told you the story pretending it wasn't her at all.

What? Of course it wasn't *me*! Look, if I wanted something from a man I would get it straight away. I don't need Tiger bloody balm.

Migraines? Well, yes, I get migraines.. What does that have to do with anything?

Reeta just laughed when we told her of Deepti's spluttering rebuttal. And we shall tell you more about Reeta too, dear reader, so you can decide whose version to believe.

But for the sake of argument, let's assume Reeta told the truth. Deepti is an independent young woman of reasonable means. Why is she afraid to admit to being in a sexual relationship?

What makes a girl grow afraid of her own body? Is it the fear of being branded a whore?

It is a legitimate enough fear. It is the fear of being disrespected; the fear of peers whispering about you behind your back, or worse, to your face; the fear of being an outcast.

The trouble is that there are never any clear rules about how you can avoid the pot-hole of brand whoredom as you ride towards womanhood. It isn't enough to be a virgin. It isn't enough to not have a boyfriend. It isn't enough to dress in salwar-kameezes and school uniforms. You can never quite know whence the next assault on your character certificate will arise. And you can never, really, do anything about it.

Buzz

Standard X, Section III, was buzzing with scandal.

Until the night of the party, it was all conjecture. Hitting Nitin with a cardboard folder? Hmm. Having her plaits pulled by Nitin? Hmm. Chasing Nitin around the field because he hit her with a book? Hmmm. But the loudest 'hmmmm!' came after Nitin's fourteenth birthday party.

Not everyone in Section III was invited. He picked ten boys and five girls, including Gaurangi, the girl who hit him with cardboard folders and whose hair he had pulled quite often.

At some point during the party, Gaurangi said to him, "I need to go to the toilet. Where is it?"

The invitees drew in a sharp, silent breath and exchanged exclamatory glances. Nobody said anything that night but next morning, all of Standard X, Section III knew that Gaurangi had told Nitin that she needed to go to the toilet.

By the end of the school-day, the whole batch buzzed.

"She just went up to him and said it, like that?"

"Why did she have to tell him?"

"She could have asked his mother or something. You don't just go up to a boy and *ask*."

"What must he have thought?"

What Nitin thought was never properly ascertained but word did get back to Gaurangi about the little sensation she had caused by making known to a boy that she needed to do intimate things like peeing.

This buzz may not have affected her had it not been closely followed by a more frightening noise. The school watchman showed up one day to complain to a teacher, claiming he had caught Gaurangi and Nitin 'in a compromising position' at the school gate, after school hours.

All hell broke loose. The watchman declined to elaborate on exactly what was so compromising about the position in which he found the two students and the rumour-mill went into overdrive. Some people whispered that they had been holding hands. Others said that the two were kissing. Some even said that he was seen taking off her panties.

Gaurangi's mother visited the school Principal and burst into tears, protesting that her daughter was one of the most innocent girls in the whole school, the whole world in fact, and the poor girl was being targeted because everyone was jealous of her indisputable beauty.

Nitin's father visited the school Principal, cleared his throat several times, shaking his head all the while, saying it just wasn't possible. His son was very focused on his studies and even Gaurangi was not a bad girl. She came from a respectable family etcetera.

Since the watchman never did elaborate on what he had seen, the buzz eventually died down. Gaurangi, however, was a changed girl. While she certainly did not stop talking to boys in the neighbourhood, she did stop telling people about the need to find a private place in which to pull down her panties and empty her bladder.

This posed no great problem for the next seven years, for she rarely found herself alone with a boy. When in mixed company, she would simply go off to look for the nearest usable toilet. She would excuse herself, saying, "One minute. I'll just be back."

A girl saying 'I have to go' or 'I'll just be back' was universally understood to mean that she was headed to the toilet. Where she came from, everyone knew this. And so, life went on.

For seven years, her luck held. Then, she met Angad.

Tall, curly-haired, research associate with an open laugh and an interest in just about everything. One fine day, he walked into the office of the NGO where she worked. She saw him, smiled at him. He looked sensitive, bespectacled and gentle and thoughtful. The sky turned bluer than blue and a hundred flowers would have blossomed if anything could have survived the dust and heat of that Delhi summer.

Gaurangi and Angad got talking. They talked a long time, exchanged phone numbers. He said, "We should catch up some time." She said, "We should." Two days later, he suggested coffee. She said she loved coffee. He took her to a café near her office.

This café, unfortunately, did not have a toilet. Once two coffees had been drunk and the conversation had lazily stretched out of the familiar zone of work and ambitions, into the sweetly personal – he liked women who wore lots of kajal and dressed in long reams of swirling fabric; she liked lean men with curly hair – Gaurangi needed to pee.

She became distracted. Her eyes swerved, looking everywhere for a door marked 'ladies' or 'loo'. Alas, there was nothing.

Angad, unable to hold her restless eyes, asked if something was the matter.

Gaurangi said, "No."

But she could barely hear anything he was saying. In this restless, desperate way, another hour passed. Angad suggested more coffee. Gaurangi refused. Tea, then? Gaurangi refused.

Slowly, the confused boy grew silent. He asked Gaurangi finally if she wanted to leave.

At this point, the girl did not trust herself to stand up and walk without embarrassing herself. So, she said, "I… umm, actually, I think I'd like to sit here a while longer. Why don't you go?"

Thus dismissed, Angad shrugged, asked for the cheque, paid, and left.

Gaurangi remained seated at the table, fighting her bladder's insistence for another fifteen minutes. She sat leaning forward, her head in her hands. When the urge receded slightly, she stood up shakily. There was a five-star hotel not far from the café and she practically sprinted across the lobby, heading straight for the rest room. Even before she could finish peeing, she burst into tears.

For a few days, Gaurangi toyed with the idea of calling Angad back and apologizing for her strange behaviour. But apologize about what, explain how?

And that was the end of the very brief love story of Gaurangi and Angad.

So a girl found herself censured for revealing her urge to urinate to a boy. Nobody could point to a rule she had broken to have created such a buzz. But what she had done called attention to her body. In her world, this was worthy of censure. Anything to do with her body needed watching, particularly those parts of her body which are supposed to be kept under wraps under all circumstances.

In most parts of the subcontinent, women – young girls particularly – will not refer to their underwear. They often have cute nicknames for the garment. In school and college we heard variations such as: the B and the P; U-Gs; inners; 'body' (perhaps a corruption of 'bodice'); slip; and 'uppers and lowers', which sounds like a reference to genres of narcotics.

In effect, the clothes you wear closest to your sexual parts are treated almost like sex itself. You keep them out of sight. If you wear clothes that allow your bra or panties to show, complete strangers – even men! – will take the liberty of telling you, so that you may rush to cover up. If you wear something that draws attention to itself, others will frown. We still haven't stopped teasing a former roommate who owned a pair of bright red panties; everybody else wore pastel colours or dark greens, browns and blacks.

In a joint family, you wash discreetly and think of how to dry lingerie with a measure of decorum. If you have male servants, you aren't supposed to let them wash 'those' clothes. Even female washerwomen might refuse to wash panties, though not for health reasons; they wash socks or negligées or pantyhose. The one thing they reject is the thing of sex.

In such a culture, what relationship does the GIG have with her underclothes?

Panty Lines

Hi. My name is Gaurangi. In the context of GIGs, I want to tell this story about panties.

We never use that word much. By 'we' I mean me and my friends and most GIGs I know. When I was little, Mummy said the word 'panty' (it took me twenty years to discover that the correct usage was plural) but as I grew up, she hesitated while saying it and by the time I was fifteen, she stopped using the word entirely. Even our hostel warden never used it. If she noticed someone's U-Gs lying out on the clothes horse, she would say sternly, "You should bring your" (and here she would pause significantly) "*clothes* inside, as soon as they are dry". But let me begin properly, at the beginning.

1. I did not think about panties – except when I'd wet them – until I was about eight years old. Then one day, my mother fired our cook, Birju. I heard her telling the left-door neighbour aunty that she found 'white' on her panties after she put them out on the washing line. I thought, perhaps it was our white detergent that hadn't been rinsed out properly. But the neighbour aunty only gasped, shook her head and declared that everyone in the colony must be told – just to make sure that nobody else hires Birju, she said. Mummy looked unhappy at the prospect of having her panties being discussed across town, but she knew it was no use telling this aunty to keep quiet. She would blab; she just had to. And so she did.

2. Wait. There was a panty-related incident, I must have been five or six years old, when I had just started taking my own baths and I used to take great pride in this, because most of my cousins were still being bathed by their mothers. Mummy would put my school uniform on the bed. I would step out of the bath in a towel and she would help me put it on.

   One day, she was busy in the kitchen and called out to me to get dressed on my own. And the next thing I remember is Mummy yelling at me for not wearing a panty. I cannot remember why I hadn't worn it. Maybe it just hadn't seemed so important.

3. At thirteen I started thinking about panties seriously when Mummy took me shopping. It was horribly embarrassing because we shopped at the stalls in the old bazaar.

   The man at the stall would pick up bunches of bras and panties in his fists, toss them up and let them fall back on his cart, all the while yelling: '*Ae pachaas, ae pachaas*'.

   Mummy told me I could pick whatever I wanted. But I just stood there, frozen. I couldn't believe she was subjecting me to the humiliation of actually touching underwear in front of a hundred people. She picked up one in embroidered beige, one plain black, and two whites, then she nudged me with her elbow and asked why I wasn't choosing my own.

   I finally pointed to a pair of bright yellow panties with white trimming. Mummy quickly set it aside, motioning to the stall-boy that this one was taken. Then she picked up an off-white bra and a yellow *chikan* one, holding both against the panties to match them. It was decided that the yellow *chikan* matched better. She smiled.

   "There's a little embroidery too. Feels nice, no?"

   She picked out another set. The white one was the standard Julie bra I'd seen on the washing lines at home. A basic cotton frame with the cups embellished with threaded concentric circles; even the straps were double-folded, starched cloth, not elastic. This 'Julie' was what most women in my mother's generation wore. If you were fancy people, you bought *chikan*-embroidered bras. The slightly adventurous aunties bought lace, flowery prints, lurid shades of lilac and magenta. Mummy stuck to white, black and beige.

4. When I was fifteen, I was sent to hostel. There weren't any washing lines outside. We all had to use wooden clothes horses. Twice a month, the chairman of the trust that ran our institute would come to the hostel. He was a man, so we had to remember not to wash U-G's that morning.
5. At nineteen, I had my first all-lace panties when Deepti's sister returned from America. She brought back lacy lingerie – she taught us how to spell and pronounce the word – for Deepti and me, her roomies. Sushila didi didn't tell her mother about the gifts she bought for us. None of us girls told our mothers either.
6. I was twenty-one when I bought my first G-string. It was off a stall in the old bazaar and it had funny moustaches printed all over it. The sort of moustache that the Air India Maharaja wears. I thought they were very cute but have worn it only once in my life. Because I had to wash it and string it up to dry, and I realized that the whole family would see it. It would be hard to explain a G-string to my family.

   Besides, they would not think that those big twirly moustaches were cute on a pair of panties.
7. I got into a fight because of panties when I was twenty-two. I had just taken up my first job, working with an NGO that taught street children. I stayed in a small room in an iffy sort of colony. There were lots of drunk, jobless men sitting around the tea stalls there. Lots of students too. There was a boy who lived across the landing, in the same building. He used to watch TV all day and half the night. Once, when the

noise went on past midnight, I knocked on his door and told him to turn down the volume.

He yelled at me and he said that he knew what kind of girl I was. He had seen my panties, hanging outside my room, on the washing line. He said, "Good Indian girls don't show anyone their panties."

8. I moved out of one iffy area into another less iffy area, bought a steel clothes horse and began to dry my underwear indoors. This worked fine in the summer. In the rainy season, clothes just wouldn't dry, indoors or outdoors. This was when I first began to iron my panties and found out that the ones with exposed elastic were no good. The elastic melted.

9. I quit the NGO and found a better-paying job, so I could move into a nicer area. This room was up on the fourth floor. I hung my washing outside, in the balcony, and there were no other buildings facing this side of the house, so it was alright to hang underwear outside. But within a month, I noticed that my panties were disappearing.

   At first, I thought it might be the maid. I was especially upset when an expensive pair in black satin went missing. I began to keep a close eye on the maid as she left the house, just in case she was smuggling out a pair of panties.

   But then one day, I was standing in the balcony looking out at the rain and noticed scraps of fabric on the dusty window ledge of the third floor. I leaned out a bit further and spotted something that looked like black satin.

   So I knew. The wind was blowing them away. But though I had located them, I never got them back. There were boys living on the third floor and I couldn't possibly go to their house and ask if they would please return my panties. There was no way I could do that.

10. I have a new maid. I don't know what she thinks about me. I used to hang my panties out on the washing line, and I took

care to pin them down with two pegs on either end, and would take them down as soon as they were dry. But soon I noticed that she had put up another washing line. This line was pressed along the wall rather than strung across the balcony. Each morning, she would quietly shift my panties and bras to this smaller, more discreet line.

I often wonder if she disapproves of me. Or if, in her own way, she is trying to protect my reputation.

11. I went into a big new store today. Exclusive lingerie store. Row upon row upon row. I looked at each closely but I didn't touch anything, although I really wanted to feel the texture of some of them. But it didn't seem okay. I kept wishing that the store didn't have a glass front.

The salesgirl came up to ask if she could help. I found myself using the fancy word – lingerie. She asked if I wanted matching sets. I just nodded at the row of panties stretched out on clip-hangers and then asked the salesgirl if she would unhook some for me. She had to ask me three times which ones I wanted, and when I told her, she asked me why I was whispering.

Gaurangi suffered (excuse the mixed metaphor) at the hands of her body but she is quick to acknowledge that she got off lightly.

Yes, there was a taunt at a delicate age, and the memory of that taunt caused her to lose a man she really, really liked, because she could not bring herself to trust him to be a different man from the adolescent idiots of her school. And it is true that that lying, over-sexed, frustrated (oh horridhorridhorrid!) school watchman almost ruined her career. But she says she is grateful that her unforgiving world accepted her back into its fold.

Perhaps, it had something to do with her beauty. She is beautiful and it is very hard to go on hating a beautiful girl. Everybody is tempted to hurt her once in a while, take her down a notch or two, show her that she isn't above anyone and must suffer her share of humiliation and pain and isolation. But it cannot compare to the punishment reserved for the not-so-beautiful.

As for the GIG with the unruly body, the one who grows up too fast and has neither academic brilliance propping her up, nor seeks out peers who might approve – God help her!

Boobs

The odd thing about Teena is that she really was one of the best girls in class. Not the best scorer of marks or even the best debater or best athlete. But she had a nice, smiling temperament and was pretty in a diffident sort of way, though chicken pox had left a few scars here and there. She was respectful to teachers and kind to her classmates. She did her homework on time and she participated in singing contests. And yet, nobody spoke of her as a particularly 'good girl'.

This was a source of some concern to her ex-best friend Gaurangi who was convinced that Teena was one of the best *persons* she had ever met. Years later, she began to suspect that the school's suspicious eye was trained upon her friend because of the way Teena was built. She had bigger breasts than anyone else in Standard VII. At thirteen, she was better-endowed than most of the teachers, and was the only girl in her class whose Saturday shirt gaped between buttons number three and four.

On Saturdays, the girls wore white shirts and pleated skorts with white canvas shoes. The boys wore white shorts. It was the sports uniform that all the students were required to wear even if they weren't practicing any sport. Nobody was complaining though. It was required that the hem of the 'skorts' be at least four inches above the girls' knees and the senior section of the school was transformed with this welcome change from a drab, loose, small-town shade of blue, into a smart display of long legs in a dazzling variety of brown. The students were also required to wear long socks, but the elastic gave way within a month and all socks rested around the ankles in a contented heap through the rest of the term. If some girl's socks refused to give way, she rolled them down.

The rest of the week, the girls wore blue tunics over pale blue shirts. On Saturday, there was no tunic veiling the girls' white shirt fronts and the budding chests underneath. Even with slips inside, anyone could tell which of the girls had breasts. That is also how one knew when a girl started putting on a bra.

Teena had not yet started. The others kept a watch on the pale outline of her half-slip under her shirt. No bra-lines. Conversations in the 11 am short-break began to centre around her torso. Ranjana and Anita were especially concerned about such unbridled growth.

Ranjana would say, "It is so odd."

Anita would say, "Why doesn't her mother do something?"

Gaurangi would say, "What should her mother do?"

They would say, "Something. It is too much!"

But her mother didn't do a thing and Teena went through the term bra-less. Gaurangi's mother, however, did swing into action. She never said anything directly, of course, but she waited until the summer break, then took the girl shopping to an underwear stall. She riffled through a heap of cotton bras and suddenly, she turned to her thirteen-year-old daughter and asked which ones she wanted to pick. That was that.

The struggle to put on a bra lasted several minutes. The hooks wouldn't get hooked, for one. Besides, Gaurangi's mother made a random decision about the fit after glancing at her chest but the tips of the cups wouldn't sit right. The last concentric circle on the white Julie eternally protested in a crumpled sort of way.

Anyway, all the girls went to school with thick, cotton slips on top of the bra. A good fit was not the first thing on their minds. They just wished everybody wouldn't notice this new extra garment on their chests.

Meanwhile, Teena still went about, breasts unbound. The third and fourth buttons still strained. Ranjana still thought Teena's mother was irresponsible for failing to take corrective measures.

One thing had changed. There was a new boy in class. Paresh had moved from a bigger branch of the same school. He was full of stories about bigger things in bigger towns. He rode a scooter although he didn't even have a learner's license. He was terrible at every sport except TT and his whole plump torso shook when he laughed, soundlessly. To top everything, he came in with a reputation of always standing first in class. Gaurangi, who was used to standing first herself, took an instant dislike to him.

Paresh lived two houses down from Teena and their mothers soon grew friendly. In school, their ease around each other was noticed.

"Teena and the new boy are very friendly," Anita said.

"Over-friendly," Ranjana sniffed.

"They are neighbours," Gaurangi interjected, awkwardly defending her ex-best friend but hating her at the same time for being friends with Paresh.

"Not quite," Anita said. "There is Sinha Aunty's house and then Bitoo's house between their houses. I should know; I live in the row behind."

"Her mother should do something," Ranjana repeated.

Gaurangi was painfully aware of the garment that was beginning to cut into the skin on her shoulders, since she had taken to tightening and raising the cotton straps on Saturdays. She didn't say anything for she felt quite bad when other girls talked about Teena.

Through Standards VI and VII, the girls had been best friends. Gaurangi was in and out of Teena's house all the time and she knew Teena's bent, old grandfather, her absent father, and her mother who baked such delicious cakes with ghee instead of butter and always chucked the girl under the chin before asking how much she weighed.

Unfortunately, the friendship collapsed because of a picnic to which Gaurangi was invited and Teena was not. These things were taken quite seriously in that colony by both children and their parents. Invitations to picnics reinforced complicated social equations. When Teena found out that her best friend had gone without her, she cooled off a little bit. Gaurangi responded by cooling off a bit more. Teena responded by not calling her over to play at her house after school. And by default, Gaurangi found herself stuck with these two girls, Anita and Ranjana.

Soon, however, there were final exams. The students moved up to Standard VIII and sections were reorganized. Anita and Ranjana went to section B and, much to her relief, Gaurangi was back in section C along with Teena.

Then, another change occurred. Nitin joined their school. He was dark, with a dazzling smile and a loud mouth. He was Paresh's cousin and lived with that family.

Despite her dislike of Paresh, Gaurangi ended up hanging out with him as part of a group: Teena, Paresh, Nitin and Gaurangi. They ate lunch together and even hung out after school hours. They talked, or played some badminton, or TT.

Paresh and Nitin's family had money and they let the boys throw parties and invite their friends, including girls. The two girls always went together. It was a good few weeks, but the bubble burst soon enough.

It began with the party at which Gaurangi asked Nitin to show her the toilet. It was enough to make the other girls think there was something going on. Tongues wagged but still the foursome hung out. That ended the day the school watchman saw Nitin walking alone with Gaurangi.

He was doing what he often did – pulling her hair or something. She smacked him on the shoulder. That was all. But the watchman complained to the school Principal that he had seen a girl and a boy in a 'compromising position'.

The matter was taken to the school Principal. Parents were summoned, explanations demanded. It was all very unpleasant but a month later, the whispers died down.

Gaurangi stopped talking to Nitin and Paresh. That year, she won the inter-school debating trophy and when the congratulations began pouring in, she felt a little more human. She began to look teachers in the eye again, talk to other students. It took a few weeks for her to realize what had happened. Everyone in class had stopped talking to *Teena*!

The 'compromising position' rumour tarnished one girl's reputation but it was another girl who got saddled with the outcast's robes. On the face of it, there was no reason for this. Both girls came from similar family backgrounds, wore the same uniform, had the same circle of friends. The difference was that Gaurangi was beautiful and stood first in class, while Teena's chest was not as polite; there was a widening gap between the third and fourth buttons on her shirt.

Teena was not unattractive but there was something wild, something off-balance about her looks. Her short, frizzy hair, limpid eyes and asymmetric teeth, her large breasts and no bra, her thick legs – the overall effect was unsettling.

Despite the social setback, Gaurangi stood first across all three sections in the second term exams. Other girls had to act friendly because they wanted to borrow her notes, or needed her help with lab experiments. Teena had nothing to offer anyone except her innate goodness. And when has innate goodness ever been enough?

Every day, Teena spent the lunch hour sitting in the school's back garden, tiffin box in her lap, head bowed, back turned to the sun. All alone.

Meanwhile, Ranjana and Anita decided to take the original outcast back into their friendly arms. They sought Gaurangi out during lunch break when everyone happily gossiped, mostly about Teena.

Anita would say, "She looks so grown up, doesn't she? Like a married woman rather than a girl."

Ranjana would say, "Her mother should do something. My mother says that in her time, they used to tie a piece of cloth round and round the chest. To make young girls look decent."

"But I've heard that it is very bad for growing girls," Gaurangi would protest.

Anita would shrug. "Well, *I* have heard that if you *don't* wear bras, you get cancer."

Gaurangi would not argue. She remembered the time Ranjana had told her that Anita had once said that *she* too looked like an 'aunty' now that she wore a bra.

Another time, the girls were sitting outside, watching Teena eat alone. Anita took a blade out of her pencil box and carefully scraped at the hair on her knee. Her mother had forbidden waxing until she cleared the tenth boards.

Ranjana nudged Gaurangi, "So she and Paresh... what happened?"

Anita clicked her tongue in reproach. "Paresh is not like that. She only was after him."

Ranjana nodded, "Yes, he is so smart. Why should he get involved with her? It makes a difference, you know, what you look like. I mean, there's nothing special about her, plus she's begun to look like a grown-up woman. But she should not be in such a hurry to become a woman."

The other two giggled a long time. Gaurangi choked on her lunch, but pretended it was because she too was laughing.

Around this time, the girls began practice for Sports Day. The students practised rough and hard. Every day, somebody would come back with an injury: sprained ankles, cramped thighs, torn ligaments, hairline fractures on fingers and thumbs. Every day, the girls would look at each other running, jumping, leaping, and between leaps, they would whisper.

"By God! It is too much now," Anita said as she watched Teena do the 100 meter hurdles.

"When she runs, she looks like such a... such a..." Ranjana trailed off.

"She's mad! Why is she taking part in the games at all? All the boys must be looking at one point only these days," Anita said.

Teena was participating in the 100 metre hurdles race and she was also on the *kabaddi* team. It was a Saturday when, during a practice session for *kabaddi,* the girls from the opposite team grabbed her, threw her down, pinned her to the floor and, in the ensuing free-for-all, four buttons got ripped off Teena's shirt.

After practice, Teena came to her ex-best friend, clutching the front of her shirt, and asked to borrow some safety pins. Gaurangi always carried safety pins, just in case a button popped or a skirt hook broke. But she happened to be sitting with those other two girls. She could see their smirks.

Teena waited, and her face stayed placid as Gaurangi lied, said she didn't have any safety pins. Anita and Ranjana couldn't help themselves. They began to snigger.

Years later, the memory stayed in Gaurangi's head – Teena, with one hand at the collar, the other pressed to her stomach, running away like one of those movie heroines from the fifties, after some tragedy has struck.

Meanwhile, Anita was saying, "I hope now at least her mother will notice. She needs to control the girl's chest."

Ranjana said, "Oh, just one bra is not enough to keep her tied down. She needs a leash."

Gaurangi stood up then and went back to her classroom. One school bag sat at an empty desk. When the last bell rang, she shouldered her own bag, grabbed Teena's bag too, and walked straight to Teena's house.

Her heart was beating loudly and she wondered if she'd faint with nervousness. She wished she could – it would be easier to be found unconscious at the doorstep rather than facing her friend and saying 'sorry'. But fainting fits don't come when they're needed. She took a deep breath, unlatched the gate, walked up to the door and rang the bell.

Teena's mother opened the door, called out to Teena and nodded at the girl – a familiar gesture that meant she should step inside. But Gaurangi stood outside, staring at her feet. Teena finally came to the door, took her school bag, whispered thanks, and went back into her room.

On Monday, during lunch break, Gaurangi took her tiffin box and went looking for Teena, who had stopped sitting in the garden because too many students stared. She found her sitting on the steps behind the library, tiffin box in her lap. Through the fabric of her tunic, the dim outline of two straps could be seen.

Gaurangi sat down on the steps. "I've brought *halwa*." She held out her open tiffin box.

Teena asked, "Why?" She didn't touch the box extended towards her.

"So you have started?" Gaurangi asked.

"What?"

"Wearing the B."

"B? Oh!"

"I started last summer."

"Really? But you don't need it."

"Mummy decided."

Teena had not yet touched the tiffin box. Gaurangi pushed it towards her and did not start eating herself until her best friend picked up the spoon and helped herself to the *halwa*.

And so the two girls were best friends again. Except that now, again, nobody in class was talking to Gaurangi!

One week of this silent treatment broke her. She went home in tears, bunked school, started making up excuses about stomach pain and back pain and headache and nausea. When she flunked the mid-term tests, her parents pulled her out and put her into another school.

Gaurangi did better at the new high school. She had new friends but she would still go over to Teena's house in the evenings. She discovered her friend was eating her tiffin alone again, hidden behind the library. And Teena ate alone until the day she left that school.

We talked to several women (and men) about GIGs. Who is a good girl, what makes her 'bad'?

It is important, a girl told us, to look good – as if your face and body were cast in a mould of balanced, controlled beauty. A good girl, in short, must not only be restrained but must also look as if she has no need for restraint, as if she doesn't even know what she is supposed to restrain and why.

Other definitions came up. Somebody mentioned baths. A GIG takes regular baths. Two a day in summer is perfect. However, if you take three or four a day, well... hmm! A few eyebrows might be raised and not just because of the wastage of water.

Yet another girl felt she had relinquished her claim to GIGdom because she smokes. "I remember thinking I wouldn't mind if my husband was a smoker but I would never smoke myself. Never ever. Famous last words. Like they say, never say never."

Why, we asked her, do you smoke? She giggles. She tells us not to make fun of her. Then she confesses it is because of her first love. First love, we ask – who?

Shah Rukh Khan, she says. "People talk of first love in a sweet, flowery, nostalgic way. Like that soap advertisement: 'Pehla pyaar laaye jeevan mein bahaar... ' *First love brings spring into your life; and this soap smells like first love etcetera. Jasmine flowers scattered across the television screen; college students blushing, all tenderness and innocence. Well, first love turned out to be nothing like its advertisement. I didn't know what to do with myself. I could not meet him. I could not have him. All I could do was smoke endlessly like him. And dream of him. I had elaborate Bollywood-style dream-sequence fantasies – me in chiffon saris or pastel dupattas; he, strong and silent. I would let my eyes do the talking; he would sing songs or play the mouth-organ."*

We keep a straight face. We do not laugh. Go on, we urge her.

"I used to think that when he met me, he would dump his wife and marry me instead. I would make him so happy! In my fantasy, I would cook parathas for him, take lunch to his film set in a tiffin box. The steel carrier type tiffin, you know? Then I read in a magazine that his wife had a baby. I didn't think it was proper to dream of him any longer."

Then?

Then nothing, she says. She got married but she still smokes – cheap, unfiltered smokes – during grocery shopping trips, or up on the terrace of her house. Nobody knows because nobody approves. "A friend found out and went berserk. 'What is wrong with you?' she kept yelling. Your lungs and your teeth and your babies and skin, blah blah. But I love that nicotine hit. Only the really cheap stuff gives you that feeling – your feet are unsteady; you feel acrid and potent."

She looked at our expressions, shrugged. "Yes, I know. Cancer. But I don't care. Everybody dies, you know. GIGs die too. And I might as well confess. It feels good to know that Shah Rukh Khan still smokes, kids or no kids. I hope he never quits. I won't either."

Does her husband know, we ask, about Shah Rukh Khan?

"What is the point of loving someone like Shah Rukh Khan if you let your husband make an issue out of it? This is a safe type of infidelity." She winks at us. "I'm having a roaring affair inside my head and there's not a thing anyone can do about it."

Well, well. Who are we to judge?

We went on asking questions. What makes a good girl feel like a good girl? What are her memories of being bad?

One girl said she felt like a GIG whenever she thought of herself as a twelve-year-old, sitting on a swing.

Another said she felt naughty when she danced – and she always looked forward to her husband's out-of-town trips so she could put on the television and copy the moves of 'item girls' who appeared in music videos, wiggling their hips and thrusting their bosoms at all who watch.

Somebody said she felt truly good when she was in the kitchen, cooking daal and rice. Somebody else talked of rain.

Rain

Hi. My name is Preeti. Let me tell you a story about rain in Rajasthan.

Rain in Rajasthan – it was rare. When it came the sky hung low, like the hem of a cotton skirt, and dripped. The drops started big, hitting the hot cement of the paved pathways with sizzling and popping sounds, then the drops became smaller, then, very suddenly, we were transported to a mini-storm, a welcome storm after all the nauseating heat and the grit of sand.

Rain in Rajasthan – how we longed for it! We went into it without our slippers, without slowing down to cover our heads and bodies, without care or grudges. Once in the rain we could not stop running. The drops were warm upon us. The ground beneath our soles was warm and delicious. Some of the girls broke into high pitched laughs. Some began to sing. Some splashed the puddles like children. Everybody ran. Our small steps took our wet bodies here and there in excitement. Rain in Rajasthan was a flower, fragranced and giddying, falling like petals upon us. The first smell of wet sand was almost unbearable in its musty intensity. The first smell of whitewashed walls. The first smell of our own bodies too, the smell of sweat, the lingering smell of perfumed shampoo and soap, and occasionally the smell of perfume itself. Who would not fall in love, in the rain of Rajasthan?

It rained and I sat upon the windowsill, watching. The rain

was not more than a drizzle and I could see individual strands of rain upon leaves and on the grid fencing. I could make out the darkened spots where drops of water had hit the sand at the end of the field. Behind the main school building another building was being annexed. Our school was to start a brand new computer department and I imagined rain upon its bare window frames, upon its unhinged doors, rain upon its unplastered walls.

Sher Singh, our school camel, appeared. He was pulling an empty cart behind him. Bhuvnesh, the cart driver, sat at the cart edge and every time Sher Singh moved, Bhuvnesh's feet swung rhythmically.

Deepti sat at my feet and I played with her short hair while she painted my toe-nails. There was an ache in my chest, a dryness, like it wanted to cry.

Bhuvnesh patted Sher Singh's back. "Aho! Aho!" he said, soothing the animal and patting its back. Sher Singh circled the school's old building and disappeared. I knew he would appear again, soon, with the cart filled with bricks.

I hummed one song after another, trying to translate my own mood into music. Occasionally Deepti raised herself on her knees and kissed me wherever she could, my arms, my lips, wherever, but I did not stop singing. I sang songs from *Jo Jeeta Wahi Sikandar* and *Jism*. I sang *Dard-e-Dil Dard-e-Jigar*. I even sang *Pyaasa Hiran* from our daily hymn book, a hymn Deepti could not bear because we sang it a million times a week, but right then she did not seem to mind. Perhaps there was pain in her too.

My notes pitched up and down, drifting like a flight of dragonflies. Then Sher Singh came again, his cart filled with bricks.

"Deepti," I said, cutting my song short. "Why are bricks always red?"

"Hmmm," Deepti said.

"Deepti, why are bricks always red?" I asked again.

She looked at me, a little unfocused at first, then a little amused. "They are red because they are red," she said. Then, "How stupid. And why have you stopped singing?"

I shook my head. "Why can't bricks be blue or yellow? Why always so drab? I hate for bricks to be red."

"You're screwed," Deepti said. "That's like asking why trees are always green."

I nodded. "Yes, like that. Why are trees always the same colour? People always brown? Why is Sher Singh always pulling the cart? Be it hot as hell or raining or cold enough to be freezing? Why are things always happening?"

Deepti groaned. "If you are in that sort of a mood I am going."

But I was in that sort of a mood so I shrugged. "Go," I said. But she did not go. She only looked at me with concern.

"Do you know how ridiculous you sound?" she said, but she was not taking me seriously. She picked up the brush and began to paint my toes again.

At other times I would have been mad at her. At other times I would have pulled my feet away, bunched them up under my chin and sulked. But today, with the sudden wind that threw the drizzle everywhere and carried the drops like mist through the window to my skin, today, with my mood and the songs still humming in my head, with Sher Singh and his circular cart, today I had no energy in my bones and I felt almost old, almost too old to be ever mad at Deepti again.

The rain was still not hard. There was still mercy in it. But the sky was rough, rougher than the wind, and I stared at it fatalistically. Some door, far away, banged repeatedly. I tried to sing another peppy Hindi number but from the corner of my eyes I could see Sher Singh and Bhuvnesh.

I could see that, like me, Bhuvnesh too stared at the sky, and the song grew heavier upon my throat. And without any warning, while Bhuvnesh and I were still staring at it, the sky cracked and then came rushing down. I stopped singing and turned to look at Bhuvnesh who had gotten off his seat and was running to the back of the cart. There was a makeshift plastic raincoat buried under the pile of bricks and he pulled at one end. He pulled hard and the piece tore off. I watched him look at the piece and I watched him throw it away, down on the ground for the rain to do what it wanted. Then he ran back to Sher Singh and stroked the camel but this time, deafened by the rain, I could not hear his "Aho! Aho!"

I watched in panic. Bhuvnesh stood beside his animal, patting its back, looking at the rain, then he took his seat and the cart started rolling again.

I felt cruelly contradicted. The red bricks, now maroon because of the water, stood humped like heaps of butchered flesh. My eyes followed till Sher Singh and Bhuvnesh turned the corner and I could no longer see them.

Neither Deepti nor I spoke. At another windowsill, Vandy and Kirti were getting ready for some singing and dancing. Rain did that – pulled out songs and dances. Even Sophie was singing. Deepti sensed my depression but I did not relax or pick up another song to hum or pretend to be happy.

"Sick," she said. It was surprising, the anger and disgust she crammed into that one word.

I shrugged. She got up and walked away and I knew everything was over between us.

"I will make up with Sarina," I promised myself, like there was no other way out. Sarina was the last person I had dumped to be with Deepti. You always have to dump somebody to be with somebody else.

I stood up and there was a new weightlessness to my step, like I could fly. I went and joined Indra, Papdi and Sophia. Now that I was free of Deepti, I could join anybody. Indra was singing, her voice husky and low. Papdi's was a simmering high tone that hit the ear drums right away. Sophia was impossibly off-tune. I started to sing again.

'A pinch of oooh, a pinch of aaaah, a pinch of your crookedness, and oh, how my heart throbs, how my heart throbs.'

I had never liked this song before but now I discovered its sauciness and was smitten. My freshly painted toes glowed. I was in love with its bright blue paint.

At another window Vandana, a.k.a Guru Vandy, was surrounded by girls sitting around her feet as she whispered philosophy into the evening.

"Philosophy is nothing but long sentences put together," she said, looking out the window and sighing. "In the West the sentence is 'You have to go looking for love for love to come looking for you'; so they go out on a quest and bring love home with them. In the East the sentence is: 'Love happens; it cannot be made to happen'; so we sit and wait for love to knock at our window."

And so on and so forth. She talked and one by one, more girls drifted towards her feet and settled down to listen. Sophia giggled.

"Hogus-bogus," she said.

When Deepti came back I continued singing, clapping and tapping and almost dancing myself. She leaned against the wall, watching me, enjoying herself. I ignored her. The dull ache within me had been replaced by an angry thud.

After I let the I-am-ignoring-you game go on long enough, she called for me.

"Hey," she said. I did not respond. "Hey. Come on," she said, shaking her head and pushing her way through the small crowd of singing dancing girls towards me. She wrapped her arms around and slightly squeezed my neck. She was grinning like a cow.

Guru Omniscient Vandy was reading out agony aunt columns from the pile of *Feminas* she had brought with her after the summer vacation. I could hear the keywords throwing her listeners into throes of simultaneous laughter and shock. "Self-stimulation," she said, "is achieved through, you know, this thing called masturbation."

I did not talk to Deepti but I stopped ooohing and aaahing and returned with her to our window. She gave my neck the squeeze again.

"Been making your famous resolutions?" she asked, and I was annoyed by the laughter in her voice.

I pushed her off. "Yes! And you stay away from me, you asshole," I said.

I could not sing anymore. The slight dejection, the tinge of depression that is so conducive to music was gone. I was happy. There was within me a sprightliness and songs were impossible. Deepti was still grinning, still laughing. She liked fighting. She loved making up, loved the after-we-make-up parts, the silly confessions and the talk of heartache.

"What all did you think of?" she asked.

"I was going to say a real stoic goodbye and have nothing more to do with you and then I was going to lure you up a cliff and push you down and kill you once and for all."

"Impressive. I was saying goodbye too, just not so stoically."

"Why did you come then?"

"You are too much of a kid to be left alone."

I rolled my eyes. Deepti was one whole year younger than me. She was only fourteen.

"I called you a *maachod* and a *baapchod* to Papdi," I said and cocked my brows.

"Those are disgusting words."

"Not any worse than Vandy's," I said. "You say all kinds of things yourself. You don't listen to me when I ask you not to."

"I am different. You are not like Vandy. You are nice. You write poetry and all."

I almost died at that one. "Poets are criminals. Don't you watch movies? Poets are murderers in movies. I don't think there is too much difference between driving a truck and writing, after a while."

Deepti frowned. There wasn't a person in the world more literal than Deepti.

I laughed. "You are stupid," I said. I loved her awfully lots. Sometimes it was so terrible.

"I don't care," she said. "Just don't be so abusive. It doesn't suit you."

"And won't life be horribly boring for me?"

"No. You are not like us. You don't need to say crap to have fun. You are so different. You frighten me with all your talks about yellow bricks and god knows what. I don't understand all that. I don't have much brains."

She looked so sad it broke my heart.

"Hey," I said and punched her slightly.

"I have spoilt you rotten. You never said the 'fuck you's before, never showed screw ups. I was thinking about that when you went to sing with those girls. I was thinking about how you were trying to tell me something but I did not know. For me red bricks are red bricks. They make durable houses and that is good enough. But I am dumb about a lot of things you talk about. If you say blue bricks are better, they must be better."

When she mentioned the blue bricks I did not know whether to laugh or cry. I slid down to sit beside her.

"Hey, what's wrong?" I asked, but she did not answer.

There was nobody like Deepti in the world, nobody so hard. We were silent for a while then I said, "You know Deepti, I was in this hostel for five years before you joined. Those were nice years. I had an awful lot of fun. I had friends, I was naughty. I was even mildly popular with boys. But I missed you. I did not know, of course, but I missed you. I think I was waiting for you, waiting for you to come be my friend, like we were back home when we were children. I think I resented you for not having followed me when my parents sent me here. But I did not know it consciously so I made other friends. It was sort of cool being linked with the coolest girl gang in school, being a part of *The Dunes*. It was great."

I picked up the bottle of blue polish and pulled Deepti's feet towards me. Her nails were not like mine. Mine were shapely, oval even on the toes, hers were so small you could hardly see the ones on her small toes. The smallest toe had a dot for a nail. It was hilarious. When I began to paint her toes looked like polka-dotted digits.

"Guys died over girls in *The Dunes*," I said, dotting one polka dot after the next. "But it was all so stupid. I hated the whole gang business with a passion. I hated your sister too. There is something awfully wrong with gangs and groups and stuffs. There is nothing in a group. Everybody hates everybody else. I don't know why I stayed at all. I didn't care a damn. I don't think anybody cared a damn."

"And Aravindum?" Deepti asked.

"I went around with him because he was good-looking and rich and because if one was in *The Dunes*, one had to go around with someone. It was a prestige matter."

I told her how it happened, how I started going around with Aravindum. "It was after summer vacation and I had come back starving in my heart. I used to get very hungry in my heart then. Very, very hungry and I used to think of dying, of twisting things into ropes and being dead. The girls didn't amount to anything and I craved a different sort of companionship, not the sort the girls gave, and not what Aman gave either. I wanted someone to call me 'Preetiness' and look at the nape of my neck while I was writing. I wanted someone to be unable to look away from the nape of my neck. And I was raving mad about Aman," I said and then stopped. "Not really. I don't really know if I was raving mad about Aman or not, but I had said that to Shushila-di one evening. It was after dinner. She and I were taking a walk downstairs. It was a beautiful evening, very silver. The wind was so cool it wasn't like Ajmer at all. The pebbles were glazed with moonlight. It was one of the perfect-est evenings I remember. I was walking with your sister and she was silver too. I guess it stirred me, the solemnity of it all. I guess I wanted it to be important. I wanted something to mark it. Or maybe it wasn't like that and I am only trying to romanticize it. I always romanticize things when I talk. I can think of things clearly, with a clear perception, but the moment I speak they get all indistinct and become lies, and yet I am not lying. I lie a lot, all the time, and yet I am not really lying. I wasn't lying then to Sushila. I was only trying to tell her about the hunger I felt and to know if she felt it too. I wanted our talk to be tragic and grand and sentimental – the evening was like that. You know how it works."

Deepti shook her head. "No clue," she said. She was not smiling now, just looking at me like I had lost my mind.

Heavy drops of rain bounced off the ledge outside the window and settled mistily upon her short hair. A few were on her lashes and she was unreal, like a sequined angel. I had never seen anyone so beautiful before that moment and for a second, when I looked at her, oval, perfect skin with a little scar above her left eyebrow, I could not stop looking. But she was looking at me too, waiting for me to go on, so I went on.

"I started talking of love," I told her, "and the more I talked, the more I talked, and the funny thing is, she and I didn't really ever talk. Maybe I was trying to make up for all the times we hadn't talked and maybe I even loved her that crazy silver evening. Whatever. Then out of the blue I said I was in love with Aravindum. I don't know why I said that. I didn't even know Aravindum. We had never spoken to one another. And yet, at that moment I saw Aravindum and how handsome he was. A tragedy slipped within me then. I thought of how I did not care a damn about Aravindum, not with all his face and his show-offy wallet. I thought of how I loved Aman instead. That was the first time the thought crossed my mind: that I loved Aman. It was so strange. I was talking about Aravindum, seeing his face before me, and I was thinking of Aman. The strangest thing was I knew both of it to be a lie. Aman was my best friend and it would be so tragic to love him even for just that – the idea that I loved Aman and Aman did not love me and he never would. I knew too that from this instant, everything between Aman and me would change. I would look at him and say to myself: I love him but he doesn't love me and everything is so tragic."

Deepti was so still I thought she had fallen asleep. Then I saw that she was playing with her feet. Her fingers gently messing the blue polish that had not yet dried. Her fingernails were small too, bitten almost to the roots and the skin above was round and bulbous. For an angel she had ugly hands and legs.

"Do you see how crazy I am? And I thought to myself I would make Aravindum my boyfriend, that it would be quite prestigious to have him as my boyfriend. And that way, Aman would remain my lonely secret. I could wear a pendant, a silver 'A' pendant and everyone would think it was 'A' for Aravindum. Only I would know it was 'A' for Aman and how fucking precious would that be! My lonely secret. Aman is my lonely secret, he really is. Sometimes I ache for him for hours and sometimes I dream of getting married to him. I dream of many, many children because he loves children. You see this band I have around my wrist? He tied it, on friendship day. Black for sexy, he said, and we laughed so much. I know I will not untie it because he tied it, and after it rots and falls off I will press it in my dictionary and keep it forever."

"That," Deepti said, finally laughing, "is sometimes called voodoo, sometimes *chudailgiri*. And your Aman–Aravindum story is straight out of loserville."

"Thank you," I said and stopped talking. Loserville, indeed.

"Come on," she said, kissing me and laughing again. "I want to know. I want to know."

So I told her the rest. Aman never found out about my love for him because Aravindum soon became my boyfriend.

"For two whole years! Damn me! And for those two years nothing terrified and irritated me as much as Aravindum did. He did weird things like once he showered bits of paper on me on which he had scribbled 'I love you I love you I love you', god knows how many times. I think he was only trying to be conventional but he surprised the life out of me. For a while, I couldn't even figure who the hell he was. I must have put him off real bad because I just didn't know how to react to his paper I love yous," I said.

"After that we never really talked. We dated during class breaks, standing behind pillars and sitting on benches behind trees, but we never knew what to say and it was so damn bleak. He always left first. He said he had to spend time with his guy-friends. I ran away to Aman and made him buy me *bread pakora* and *chhola*. I don't know what Aravindum made of the whole thing. I think he knew I loved Aman. Anyway, I wrote Aravindum long and gross love letters and gave him extra large valentine cards. He took them, of course, but he looked at me strangely. He never gave me cards except during our first year. What do you think he thought of me, Deepti? What do you think? I think it was pretty dreadful."

"I think you are crazy," Deepti said.

"Crazy! Hah!" I said. "I am crazy. Do you know that? I am totally crazy. What if Aman should come and propose to me one day? I think he is slightly in love with me. I think so and Shushila-di thinks so. Shushila-di thinks he is jealous of Aravindum. I think so too. I think he might come propose to me any day now. I am sure he will propose to me before we leave school and he will propose to me seriously. He has been very tight and snappy of late. I told you about the canteen incident, didn't I? Oh yes, he will come any day now. I dream of it often, the day he will propose to me. It will be such fun! It will be fun to experiment kisses on him. Yes? I think if I kiss him I will be nostalgic about it for the rest of my life. You know how they say the first kiss and the first touch and god knows what not. Do you know I am crazy about him? Do you know that?"

Deepti stared at me. It was getting darker outside and the lights in the corridor came on. A shard of yellow light split and shone golden on the atomic drops of mist upon her hair and lashes and on the crescent scar above her brow and inside her eyes. Her eyes were brown, only shades darker than her skin.

"You are a nutcase," she said. Then she asked me if she was my next Aravindum. "Am I the person you spend your class breaks with?" she asked.

"Aravindum!" I laughed. "Ha ha! You are not Aravindum at all. Aravindum was a bore. You know how it ended between us? One day he said he wanted it over, that it made him very angry to be with me. I said all right. I was relieved as hell to have the whole thing done with anyway. Aravindum was such a bore. But there was Aman to think about, you know. Aman really thought I cared about Aravindum. He could never have thought anything else. Had it not been for Aman, I could not have cared a damn about that snotface Aravindum, but there he was. There was always Aman. So instead of saying 'All right', I started to cry, and once I started to cry I just kept on crying. I have never cried like that in my life before. It scared Aman stiff. Poor Aman. He kept trying to be funny but I feel guilty about it now."

I looked at Deepti, her soft face, her soft hair, her soft tummy. Everything was soft about her, her hands, her ugly legs, her pretty lips and ears.

"How mad of you to think you are Aravindum. How can you ever be Aravindum? You are my Deeptikins. My own Deeptikins. You know I am crazy about you, don't you? Totally, madly, unconditionally crazy about you. I have never been so crazy about anything in my life. I will not be nostalgic for Aman's kiss. I want it very much, that kiss, but I will forget it. I will probably forget Aman too, with time, though I will ache for him all my life. But I know if I kiss you I will be nostalgic forever, it will never go away. I know I am already nostalgic for you; there is already a tragedy between us. You are that silver lining I look for in every evening. No evening ever satisfies me because I look for it in each one of them.

"Do you know that I will never be happy again because I will look for you in everything? You can never imagine my loneliness. You cannot. You never will. And that is why I hate you. Do you know how much I hate you? How much I curse you within my heart? How I want to go back in time and erase everything you have touched and looked at? My life would be perfect if I could erase you. Everything would be. But now nothing will ever be right."

"You are a psycho," she said and I felt the crush of sudden anger within me. Suddenly I could not bear her. Her stupid, simple ways of thinking. Her stupid simple way of living her life. Wake up, brush your teeth, eat, and fucking sleep. Repeat. Repeat.

"*You* are a psycho!" I cried. "You are stupid and selfish and petty. You think I worship you, don't you? You think I would die without you. But I don't. I hate you. That is all. I fucking only hate you."

"One day I will record all the things you say and make you hear them. You don't know what crap you talk."

"What do I care?" I said, the anger gone too, just like that. "What do I care? One day I will be out of school and then nothing will matter anyway."

We were quiet and during the silence I was afraid again of Deepti, of who she was, of her straight, unknotted mind.

"Deepti," I said.

"Hmmm?"

"Say something."

But she was laughing. She thought I was talking because I loved talking and that was true too. I was talking because I loved talking but I was not raving and for once I was not lying. She laughed loudly, as though at a badly told joke, and she held my cheeks in her palms and shook her head, her eyes filled with disbelief.

"It is a good thing I don't understand your language," she said. "It is blue bricks to me but I love you and your bricks and what not.

But I love you, okay?" She said it like it was the most natural, the most plausible answer.

It was dark now. The rain was a drizzle again. In the sky small patches of blue showed, the colour of our toes. The wind brought a few more drops and dappled my arms. And Deepti loved me.

Sher Singh pulled another load of bricks to the construction site and Bhuvnesh stroked his long neck and clucked at him and said something in a language only camels understand. And the rain, the one that fell on our desert, took my madness away and left me calm.

Love – who has escaped its sting?

Yet, the average GIG doesn't seem to spend that much time trying to figure out what love is all about. Sure, she falls in love. And she denies love too; she transfers and transmutes love from one subject to the next. But to philosophize about whether or not love is a myth, or how one can categorize the different genres and sub-genres of emotions that pass for love… it is a tedious, charmless process.

The average GIG has far more important questions to wrestle with. For instance, who should one love? What to do if the beloved is a girl? What if the beloved is also a boy? And what if you cannot decide who to love more?

happiest if it was the same man for both of us. Because then she'd know exactly what was going on in my mind and my body. I think that's probably what she wanted.

I don't know what *I* wanted. But I wanted to keep Kartik out of our discussion; out of that bed.

I lay very still, staring up at the ceiling, flat on my back, giving off what she called 'negative vibes.' And she lay very still too, staring at the ceiling, flat on her back.

This is what I thought of as our Kumbhakaran pose – we'd be flat on our backs, hands listless by our hips, chins against the world and death in our eyes. We'd be very still, even when we were awake, as if struggling to capture the last night of peace, before tomorrow and its strange battles between good and evil. We lay awake, knowing why Kumbhakaran slept so long.

As we lay, not looking at each other, our security melted into a battleground's premonition of the morning after. The bed was turning into a stage set for diplomatic hostility. I knew that if I moved even half an inch, this way or that, I'd be breaking a very fragile status quo, either initiating cold war, or else, opening the door to further cross-examination – depending on whether I turned away, or towards her.

So I lay, staring straight up, wondering whether I should breathe slower and deeper, let her assume I'm asleep. But just then, Mehek turned over, facing away from me. Now *I* was getting 'vibes', and I knew they were meant to be negative.

I was always miserable if she faced away before we'd fallen asleep. It was such a war-like pose. Besides, we had planned on an early breakfast at the German Bakery; a hostile bed meant no sleep and no warm pastries for breakfast. It meant getting up too late in a bed that was still smoking with anger. That is, assuming I could fall asleep.

I cannot fall asleep with an angry person. So I desperately wanted her to turn over. If she'd just come back to status-quo –

preliminary-tentative position of staring at the ceiling, lying side-by-side – I could find something to say so that she wouldn't be angry. In fact, now I was hoping she would ask about Kartik, so I'd have something to tell her.

But Mehek didn't turn over. I could hear us breathe. I could hear the clock tick. She was breathing deep, which was a sure sign that she was pretending – she never breathes deep when she's asleep – her heart usually races and I can almost feel the throb of her dreams against my shoulder. But she was facing away and I was wide awake.

I considered touching her arm, or slipping an arm around her. But I was too frightened. No, I was too proud. Or was it really pride? Perhaps, it was righteous annoyance – what business was it of hers what I do with a man? Why should she try to worm it out of me? And why did we have to make all our plans together? Why should I have to lie when all I wanted was to be left in peace to fall in love with a man, just like other girls?

Each question raced through my head, hard on the heels of the other. Yet, I dared not move. If I turned to face the opposite wall now, it would mean a confirmation of hostility. And I was too proud to turn towards her or curve along her body, so that we were now two concentric half-circles that are neither angry nor complementary. Like a foetus within a foetus – not protective, merely conceived through some freakish unending circle of fertility that couldn't find its way to fruition. Like two sprouting beans. Or like the logo of some expensive clothing brand.

The silence grew thicker, greyer. My back grew stiff with the effort of not turning over. I could not think of what to do. So I sighed. Deeply. Loudly. Sadly.

As if on cue, Mehek turned over, back to the stare-at-ceiling position. I turned my head a little to look at her. Her eyes were open. I continued to look at her, until she too turned her head to face me.

Relinquishing of immediate hostilities. Ceasefire. She reached over and adjusted the mosquito-net above my pillow. "You never tuck it in properly. The mosquitoes always get in."

"That's not my fault. There are holes in the net."

"I know. I need a new one. I'll tell Papa."

We'd both have felt infinitely better if we could get the dynamics of sleep right. If we could just have tossed and turned a few times, quickly, as if finding comfort points in the mattress, and then settled into a face-to-face curl. Like a supplicant looking into his own begging bowl. Like a concession and a grant and a willing ear.

Or a pillow under her stomach, her head turned towards me, turned over on my side, as if precariously balancing along the edges of a truce.

But neither of us wanted to be the first to grant the concession and neither of us wanted to extend the hand that held the begging bowl of an apology.

So I tried the half-way truce of a diagonal. I twisted my knees away from her, drawing my head closer to hers so that I was staring across the room – not at her, but not away from her either. She responded by turning her knees towards me but with her head and arms twisting away from me, so that she was also looking diagonally across the room. Both of us stared at the same junction of wall and ceiling for a few seconds.

This was better. Not a happy entwining but the bed was no longer like the university campus during elections. All we needed now was words – words that shimmy into the crevices of a spat; laughter bubbling up through the piped steam of words that won't mean a thing next morning; words to cement a freshly-made ceasefire.

I said, "Mehek?"

"Hmm?"

"Do you think god is a virgin?"

She rolled over onto her stomach. "Do I think god is a virgin? Well, it is possible. We do worship the *kumari*." Her eyes were beginning to dance; I could see even in the grey blindness of the mosquito-nets. She added, "But it all depends, doesn't it?"

I uh-huh-ed.

"It depends on god's gender," she went on. "If god is a woman, it is likely that she is a virgin. Because only a virgin who has no clue how great sex is would think about forbidding it outside of marriage."

"Ah! That, coming from a virgin?"

"But I'm not an intellectual-moral virgin. See, even scientists agree that sex is all in the mind. Sex is always on our minds. So that means, you and I are only technical virgins. Our minds have been led astray long ago into the deepest pits of moral depravation where we've already found our spiritual homeland. Now it is just a question of finishing the physical act."

"But what if he is a man?"

"Then the chances are that god is not a virgin. Men can't do without sex."

"And you would know this, how?"

"See, if a man has not had sex, he will never admit to it. It's an ego thing. They like to boast. So, if god is a guy, he would be the last person on earth to pretend to be all holy and pure. In fact, if god was a man, he would have sent us scriptures saying that everyone – the women especially – should have plenty of sex. That way, there'd be a greater chance of everyone getting lucky."

I had to smile. Kartik complained bitterly about girls like me allowing a false moral code to repress their sexuality, thereby making the whole world an unhappier place. But I didn't want to bring Kartik into the conversation.

I said, "So, if he is a man, who would he have sex with? A woman?"

"Who else?"

"I don't know. The houris?"

"There are no houris. If there were any houris, god would never have created women."

I thought again about Kartik and his crazy ideas. He believed in houris, he said, even if he did not believe in god or religious strictures or heaven and hell. Houris were his last hope, he used to tell me, for they were women who could love a man without any foolish hopes of marriage or children.

"You know what?" I told Mehek. "I think houris are prostitutes who make it to heaven."

Mehek sniggered. "Houris are supposed to be virgins."

"Maybe they are also like us. Only technical virgins."

She laughed. "Maybe!" she said. "At any rate, we are agreed on one thing – God is not a well-settled boy with good character, traditional family values and a five-figure salary."

We both dissolved into giggles.

"But, but, but," she said. "One thing I want to know is – who initiated god into sex?"

"Nobody. He's god. He created it. Maybe that's why it's such a clumsy deal," I said.

"How would you know? Sex is only clumsy for novices like you," she retorted. "But think about poor god. Was he nervous when he created sex? And who seduced god?"

"I don't think he needed any seduction. Who would dare seduce god?"

"So what would god do if he wanted sex?"

"Well," I said, "if god has made man in his own image, then it is reasonable to conclude that god masturbated. Maybe man was created when god masturbated."

Mehek laughed so hard the bed shook.

"I know! Woman was created because man, who was created in god's image, kept wanting someone to, you know, lend a hand."

The lights in the next room, where Mehek's father and mother slept, came on. Aunty's voice was irritable. "What's the matter? Not asleep yet?"

We were both kicking up our feet in the air now, pillows pressed over our mouths, stifling our laughter lest the whole household woke up. When the lights in the next room were switched off, I began whispering again.

"Seriously, if god ever wanted to have sex, what are his options?"

"None. At least, according to the concept of 'one god' or a god without a body. Hindu gods are much better off. They have bodies and avatars and there are plenty of goddesses and apsaras around. The gods in other religions have it bad. There is nobody around except angels. God can't have sex with angels. There must be caste barriers and all."

"True. Besides, angels are painted as cherubic, winged babies... he wouldn't want to have sex with them."

"Of course not."

"Maybe that's why he takes avatars." She sat up, unable to lie down with the excitement of this thread of thought. "Maybe god is polygamous, because he takes his pick of beautiful women and he builds a huge harem. And he calls them houris or apsaras or whatever."

"Or maybe he is a woman after all."

"Maybe he is a jealous god. He doesn't want any sexual competition in heaven. Maybe that is why there are only apsaras and houris, all very sexy women. Angels have no sexuality."

"How can you be so sure?"

"Oh come on! Can you imagine angels having sex?"

I tried to imagine it and promptly burst out laughing. The lights came on once again in the next room. We buried our faces in the pillows again, surfacing only when the light was switched off.

"Shivashivashivashiva..."

"Taubataubataubatauba..."

We both pinched our ears and turned to look at the picture of Buddha hanging near the door. I said, "He has probably got his eyes shut because he's so embarrassed living with you. The sort of things he hears in this room!"

"I'm sure he's got his eyes closed in sheer pleasure. Besides, he doesn't have my sympathy. He abandoned his wife and kid."

This was a touchy point with Mehek. She was into Buddhism these days but was not so forgiving of the prince who chose meditation over his own family. Mehek was big on family. Her mood had already turned dark.

"The gods do anything they like. It isn't fair. They can do incest, adultery, cross-dressing, polygamy. They can do anything. The rules only apply to us."

I decided to change the subject.

"God has no gender, Mehek. No rules apply because he can turn into anything, man, woman, beast, combination of the above," I said. "If god is a sexual force, then it must be a bisexual force. In fact, why just bisexual? He could be multi-sexual. He could be all sex."

I was again thinking of Kartik. The way he went on about sex, the human need for sex, the high aims and purifying properties of sex – it was almost like a religion. He considered it a basic human right.

Mehek's mood had not lifted. She was still grim. "You know what, Ruby? I think this world is one big, twisted adolescent fantasy in some god's mind. That's why humanity is the way it is. It's all fucked up and no matter what we do, we all end up feeling screwed."

Unsmiling, we both stared at the dark ceiling. Until Mehek said, "So what have we decided? Is god a virgin?"

God, sex, love, food, laughter – these are commonplace passions. A GIG talks about why foreign cornflakes cost so much more or she might debate the merits of Bata sandals over dubious booty in flea markets. But her most intimate conversations are always about god and men. Because even the most unquestioning, self-centered GIG notices that the world is not quite right.

What kind of creator would make a world like this where people are born only to plod painfully towards death? What kind of love or respect is she to offer a god who allows a loveless fate for so many people? And what kind of god bestows the gift of life, the gift of sex, upon men who assault little girls?

What can a GIG do, even if she survives such a world, except poke fun at the gods who willed her destiny?

Virgins: 2

Hi. My name is Teena.

About GIGs, I can tell you many things but first, let me tell you of one little incident from the time when I was at college. I shared a room with Deepti, Padma and Gaurangi. We all met in the hostel, though I knew Gaurangi from school.

One night, we began to play our old game of secret-swapping. Deepti told us about being fifteen kilos heavier, and how she used to steal *laddoos* from her grandmother's larder. Padma shocked us all thoroughly, although we pretended to be cool about it, when she told us about running away to marry her dad's chauffeur. Gaurangi told them about those horrible weeks when she thought she might get expelled because that idiot watchman saw a boy pulling her plaits.

I started to tell them about that boy who begged and begged to become my boyfriend when I went back home in the holidays. He had even jumped off from the roof of our old school library, just to prove his love for me. But suddenly, I broke down.

I cried for so long that the girls were petrified. They took turns at putting their arms around me, patting my head, asking what the matter was. Was I actually in love? Did the boy die?

And before I could stop myself, I had blurted it all out. About Chacha-ji and what he had been doing for the last eight years. I told them everything, about how I had begged my mother to send me to boarding school, and how worried I was that I could no longer escape Chacha-ji because my father had retired and had gone back to the ancestral house with his other brothers.

They listened, stunned into silence. Then they told me not to worry. They invited me to come over to their homes during the holidays so I did not have to meet that bastard uncle of mine. Gaurangi was particularly upset that I had not confided in her before, although we had been best friends once.

Later that night, the electricity conked off. It was nothing new. Usually, all the girls in the hostel would step out of their rooms and sit outside on the cool marble floor of the corridor. The windows were left wide open to let in as much fresh air as possible.

I didn't feel like stepping out so I pretended to be asleep. The three of them sat outside and whispered just outside the window of our room. Despite myself, I strained to listen.

Deepti was saying how awful it was. Padma was fretting about how I would manage once I graduated from college.

Then I heard Gaurangi say, "But it is not like it makes such a difference any more. I mean, once somebody has done it to you, what difference does it make?"

A week later, when I was returning to the room after a bath, I overheard Gaurangi saying, "But she's not a 'girl' girl now, is she?"

I knew at once that she was talking about me.

One month later, during the Diwali break, Chacha-ji showed up at the hostel. He said my father had sent him to fetch me home. We would be taking a train the next morning and he had made arrangements for us to spend the night at a hotel.

The girls told me not to go. They said I didn't have to. I could spend the holidays in their houses. Gaurangi was very insistent. But finally, I went with my uncle.

I know what my roommates thought, and perhaps, still think: that I was a bit of a whore for going home with my Chacha instead of accepting their invitations to come to their homes and live unmolested for a few more months. But they already thought what they thought about me. How could I go and live in their homes, talk to their parents and sleep and laugh and pray and celebrate, all the while pretending to be a good, innocent girl, just like them?

In the news lately: a Swedish couple's practicality is being questioned because they have so far refused to place their two-and-a-half-year-old child in any gender bracket. The child's name is Pop. Pop plays with dolls and cars, and Pop sometimes wears trousers, sometimes skirts. Public opinion is divided. Nobody knows what to make of the whole issue but the parents are convinced that they are actually protecting Pop from all the gender biases that exist in society.

Makes you wonder, doesn't it, how India would turn out if everybody's gender was kept secret until... well, until breasts and beards made them obvious.

Would one feel the need to constantly guess at what's inside the pants, or would nobody want to know? And how, then, would we fall in love?

Words

Hi! This is Preeti here again.

So you want to know how it ended – the troubled love of Deepti and Preeti? Oh well, you might as well know.

We learnt our words from Vandy. One semester we were word-innocent, the next our minds were swarming with forbidden diction. Masturbation. Fuck. Erection. Lesbian. Gay. We gasped and giggled at each word, our hearts beating wildly within us. We re-read the agony columns and this time understood so much more, now that we had words to aid us.

We now had words to label our own selves too. Our unnamed secrets, the ones we indulged in after everyone else had fallen asleep, took on new meanings. Our pleasures, already tainted with guilt, became more difficult to bear. Even as Vandana went into a marathon about the details of 'stimulations', some of us fell silent and participated by not participating. It was a dicey situation. On the one hand, we were afraid of the words we were learning; on the other, we were relieved to know we were not the only ones doing 'sick' things.

I finally became too afraid the day Vandy defined lesbians. "Lesbians are girls who love girls," she said, and I wished she would stop and never speak again.

But Vandana spoke almost all night long and the girls hung on every syllable. I lay in bed with Deepti next to me. We both pretended to be asleep but I knew from the way she was a little stiff that she was awake. A kind of death settled upon me then and I felt the weight of rocks inside my stomach. I wanted Deepti to turn towards me and laugh at Vandy, but she did not turn and I knew that if I ever lost Deepti, it would be to a word.

There is a song sung by women just before a marriage begins. It is a warning to the groom, playfully tuned, lines added at whim, laughter and grunting encouraged through its rendition. There are many songs sung through the course of a marriage ceremony, but this one song makes the groom laugh and shiver all at once.

Sun ré dulha, I will torture you endlessly
And over the course of time
I will invent petty crimes
And pester and harass and hassle and go on at it
Till you long for long lonely walks in the woods

Sun ré dulha, I might even curse your day and say
— Oh, you nogooder, your boss will never promote you to a better position
— Oh, you nogooder, I would rather that you be dead than that I wed you tonight
— Oh, you nogooder, may your hair stick out and your pants fall off and a hundred other horrid things happen
— Oh, you nogooder, the bed will never creak and the pots will never bang and perhaps this night will never pass

Sun ré dulha, all my life I will make you blush at my shamelessness
And my bawdy words
And my slang
My dirty jokes will send hysterics up your spine
And my revenge will make you weep!

Sun ré dulha, I come to you veiled
As a snake hides beneath the grass.

Men

Deepti felt a little like the princess in the fairytale – the one about a pea and a huge pile of mattresses. Here she was, sitting on top of fifteen mattresses, ensconced between half a dozen pillows, in a rented house three houses from her own.

This house had been rented for a week to accommodate the barrage of relatives that were coming out the collective family ears: down they poured, off the dusty shelves of Sabaila, Rampur, Sitapur; they swam across continents, from Dubai and London, weaving their way through the narrow gullies of Benaras. These mattresses had been hired for them, as had been the pillows, extra sheets, folding beds and chairs. Tomorrow, Pappubhai Tent-wale would supply the colourful *shamiana* and carpets for the *mehndi* ceremony, and the day after, Sushila would be married and would leave the house.

It had been Sushila's idea – coming to this room, clambering on top of the mattresses, jumping up and down, shooing away all other cousins. She had slid off the pile a minute ago and she was returning now, a little breathless, eyes shining, carrying paper and pens.

"So, what list is this?" Deepti asked.

"A list of men," her sister replied.

"Men?"

"Yes, we're going to make a list of all the men in our lives so far."

"But I haven't *had* any men in my life, as such."

"*Arre,* not like '*having*' having. I mean, any boy you went out with. One who likes you. Somebody who touched you," and Sushila's soon-to-be-wedded eyes took on a shiny, naughty edge. "Somebody *you* wanted to touch?"

This is what comes of getting married too young, Deepti thought, and vowed not to be married before she had had at least three proper affairs. Poor Didi, making all these lists of men in her life when there really hadn't been any proper relationships.

Even though Sushila had gone to America for two long years, she had come back single, much to her parents' relief, and to her sister's eternal disappointment. She hadn't reported having had a single boyfriend. Nothing!

There was Nick, of course. But Nick wasn't, strictly speaking, a part of Sushila's life. He was in all their lives as the son of family friends. He often took the girls out – both of them – and Deepti had seen the way he looked at her sister. She had watched her sister blushing under his scrutiny, and had examined the gifts and Archies cards that had begun arriving at an accelerated pace. This year, he bought her a solid gold bracelet for her birthday.

The whole family had gasped when the presents were opened. The girls' parents had a serious, whispered conference that night. Two months later, Sushila was introduced to and engaged to Vinay – son of a marble quarry owner from Jodhpur, a well-educated, very modern fellow who loved the idea of marrying a girl who had studied abroad. Vinay suited their forward-looking post-graduate daughter just fine. Nick of the different religion was quickly set aside.

Now, as the rest of the house was being swept and mopped and de-cobwebbed in preparation for the wedding, Sushila and Deepti had retreated into this corner where the mattresses for the guests were stored.

They pored over their A4 sheets, chewed their pens and frowned as they recollected.

Deepti, strictly speaking, didn't have a 'past'. She had tremendous aspirations, of course, but her idea of an 'affair' was limited to going out with boys to nice coffee shops and movies without telling anybody at home. If she just thought of a boy as somebody she might introduce to her family, just having this thought would count as a full-blown affair in her mind.

Currently, her list included the names of all the boys who had caught her fancy (five), those she had spent one afternoon drinking coffee with (three), of which she had held hands with one. There was one whom she fallen pretty hard for (but who hadn't paid her any attention), two who had fallen hard for her (but were not good-looking at all), and two more who had been following her home every day for the past two years (they rode on bikes, side by side, quite content not to compete aggressively in a fine show of solidarity). There had been one guy, a classmate who stood outside her house at two o'clock in the morning, swearing he would kill himself if she didn't come out to meet him right away. And that was all.

Deepti finished writing, bounced gently on the mattresses and dust flew into her nose, making her sneeze. Biṭṭu, their younger cousin from London, entered the room and asked what they were up to. She shooed him away.

"We're making lists. Go away."

"I want to come up there."

"No. Not now."

He tried to clamber onto the mattresses but Deepti stood up threateningly.

"Don't argue! We're elder to you, aren't we? It is rude to argue with your elders. Get out."

"What? I can't even sit in the room?"

"No."

She pushed him out and locked the door. As she returned to her place, she noticed that Sushila was still working hard on her list. Were there so many names? Besides Nick, who?

When she was finally done, Sushila grinned and bit her tongue.

"You go first."

"No, your list looks longer. You go first."

"No, it was my idea. You first."

Deepti went through her list quickly. Her sister was familiar with most of the names anyway. The classmate, sadly, the whole family knew about, thanks to the 2 a.m. fracas in full public view, as he stood there screaming that he loved her and she couldn't do this to him.

On Sushila's list, the surprise item was 'Khanna uncle'.

"Him?"

"He kissed me once."

"*What?*"

"I'd gone to play at Nishi's house and I needed to use the bathroom. She told me to use the one in her parents' bedroom because the flush wasn't working in hers. So, I went to that bedroom and Khanna uncle was in his bedroom. After I used the loo, he began to talk to me… school and the annual day function or something. Then he kissed me and said he was very fond of me."

"What did you do?"

"I didn't know what to do. He asked me if I minded his showing me some affection. I didn't know what to say, so I said, 'no'. He said, 'good', and then I left the room."

"Did you tell Nishi?"

"Yes."

"What did she say?"

"She said men are like that. I shouldn't trust any man, not even her father."

Deepti shuddered. She knew that her sister's friendship with Nishi had cooled but hadn't known why. And to think that *that* Khanna uncle had actually attended the engagement party!

Then Sushila went back to scanning her list.

"This is a double item: Rajan and Pavan. Pavan used to be in my physics tuition classes."

"What's the story? Why didn't you tell me before?"

"Because I was so confused and so embarrassed."

Deepti's brows went up.

"No, no. Nothing like that. The thing is, I had developed a crush on both these guys. Simultaneously. Don't laugh!"

"I'm not laughing."

"You're laughing."

"I'm not. Swear to God."

"How it all began is a little fuzzy. Pavan insists that I was the one who started it. I smiled at him on the first day. Then Pavan started sending all sorts of forwards on email. We started chatting a lot. He was witty. And he had this way of sounding like he really cared about you, you know?"

"This was going on while you were going out with Nick?" gasped Deepti.

"Oh hello! I was never 'going out' with Nick. He's a family friend, remember? Anyway, so Pavan and me, we told each other things. College, my sister's best friend, his brother getting into bad company. Then one day, I got an email from a complete stranger. His chat name was 'dood' and he said he was a friend of Pavan. He saw me on Pavan's friend-list and decided that he too would like to be my friend."

"And you said –?"

"At first, I didn't say anything. I asked Pavan and he said his friend Rajan had been asking a lot of questions about me. So I added 'dood' to my chat. I think Pavan was a little upset but he didn't say anything. I chatted with both. Sometimes, I used to keep wondering if they were sitting there together, maybe at the same computer, comparing how I chat with each one. So, I started making the conversations different. With Pavan, I was more friendly, talking of myself and my family. With Rajan, I was vague – studies, politics, stuff like that. Still, after a month, I began to feel like I was attracted more to Rajan."

"Attracted? Just from chatting?" Deepti's incredulity was writ large on her face.

"He seemed funny, also a little wicked, you know?"

"He had to be wicked. To just start talking to some girl on chat!"

"Listen, *na*. Looks-wise, Pavan is nice – tall and fair. But I didn't know what his friend looks like. I was chatting blind. Then finally, Rajan said he wanted to meet me in real life."

"Don't tell me you agreed."

"No. First, I only gave him my phone number. He called and gave me his number. We talked on the phone a couple of times and he asked if I would like to come home."

"Home?"

"Home."

"Didi, tell me you didn't."

"Not alone. I did a smart thing. I said, okay, why don't I ask Pavan to bring me over because he must be knowing your address quite well?"

"That was not a smart thing to do, Didi. It is dangerous. Two boys you don't know, in a house you don't know-"

"*Arre*, listen," Sushila interrupted. "He also said, okay. So we all met. He ordered pizza."

"Then?"

"Then nothing. But then, a day later, Pavan asked me to meet him somewhere outside. Not in tuition class. So I said, where? He said, my place. And it was really awkward for me because he lives with two other boys in a rented room. I didn't want to go. But I had already visited Rajan's place, so if I refused to go to Pavan's place, it would seem like I didn't trust him. Even though he was the one who was my friend first, before I met Rajan. You see?"

"So did you?"

"I went."

"Shit! Alone?"

"What could I do? It would be too much if I asked Rajan to come along. You know, it would be too obvious if I kept asking one guy to come with me to visit the other guy's place. They would know I don't trust either one."

"Didi, you are really so stupid," Deepti groaned.

"*Arre,* listen to the story first. Then Pavan did a bad thing."

"What did he do?"

"When I went to his room, he was there, just lying on the bed. I didn't know where to sit. I didn't want to sit on his bed, so I cleared a corner on his side-table and sat there. He said, 'Make yourself comfortable'. I said, 'I'm fine, I am comfortable here'. He said, 'You can put your feet up and sit properly on the bed'. But I stayed where I was. I couldn't possibly sit on his bed while he's lying down on the same bed, could I?"

"Of course you can't!"

"He should have known that. I was quite upset. He should have sat upright at least, *na*? But that's not all."

"No?"

"I don't know how but somehow, we began to talk about dating and then, guess what!"

"What?"

"You won't believe this. He asked me what my opinion was on the subject of one-night stands."

"Whaaatt?"

"Imagine! I was left with my jaw hanging open till here!" Sushila said, pointing to her ample cleavage.

"Then?"

"Then what? I almost choked. Finally, I told him, I would never consider such a thing. He started saying that there was nothing wrong with it, blah blah, just two people who are attracted to each other blah blah and freedom of choice and false morality blah blah… you know, the usual stuff."

"So then?"

"Then I said I have to go home. We didn't talk so much in class after that, and soon after, I stopped chatting with him."

"Phew! So that was the end?"

"More or less."

"But what about Rajan?"

Sushila grew pensive and was quiet for a few seconds.

"Something strange happened. Some anonymous guy sent me an email saying he was in love with me. He knew all kinds of things about me: how I looked, how I walked, where I studied, what my routine was. Deepti, I can't tell you how scared I was. I was shit scared. Two days later, he sent another email. Finally I wrote back. I said, 'I'm not interested, please leave me alone'. And he went berserk. He hacked into my email and sent filthy, abusive mails from my ID to my friendlist. Then he deleted the entire address list."

"My god! What a creep!" Deepti shuddered. "Was it Rajan?"

"I don't know. Deepti, I don't want to believe that. But the tone of the emails, the style, it was the same. I only know him only from his internet talking style, after all."

Sushila sighed. "I have stopped using that email address and he too has not tried to contact me again. I can't believe that I actually thought I liked him, once." She sighed again.

Finally, Deepti broke the silence. "Didi, is Rajan good-looking?"

Sushila shrugged.

"Is he tall?"

"Yes."

"Fair?"

"Yes."

"Lips?"

"Full."

"Smile?"

"Easy."

Deepti sighed. Sushila sighed.

"Is there anybody else left on your list?" Deepti asked, hoping fervently that there wasn't.

"Well, there's Sid."

"Who is this Sid now?"

"I met him on the internet. There was this dating website I used to surf in America."

"And you signed up, just like that?"

"Well –"

"Didi*!* You are really a little too forward!" Deepti paused to let her disapproval sink in. But she couldn't stop the curiosity that was eating her up. "So how long did that last?"

"Well –"

Deepti's brows were rising steadily skyward as Sushila chewed demurely on the end of her pencil.

"Don't tell me! You are still … ? *Didi!*"

There is this little girl. Her name is Divya. She is eight years old and already has some inkling of what a good girl is. But before getting into the nitty-gritty of her life choices, let us analyze the good girl's dilemma.

A good girl is simultaneously taught three very contradictory facts:

a) A girl can never be a boy.

b) It is all right for a girl to be like a boy sometimes but it is NEVER all right for a boy to be like a girl.

c) Since it is a man's world, ultimate victory is achieved when a girl can behave like a boy, at least at a professional level.

A girl of eight may not yet understand why she can never be a boy or how her professional goals should be defined but she does see the disadvantage of being allowed to be like a boy.

Divya's brother, Deep, is a year younger. However, sister and brother are almost the same size. The result is that Divya has to wear Deep's clothes. Or rather, Divya and Deep wear clothes that are suitable for Deep.

Since Deep cannot wear frilly frocks or tie his hair with deliciously coloured ribbons, Divya is saddled with stack after stack of checked shirts and baggy pants, in earthy tones. Her hair is cut short too to suit her sartorial style. There is a row of multi-coloured sneakers to choose from and for accessories, there's an assortment of belts.

One can only imagine Divya's heartache as she watches her peers prance around in knee-length dresses and snow-white sandals (some of her classmates are even allowed to wear nail-polish).

She is not sweet, not in the conventional sense. She is not someone you want to cuddle and she is already too ambitious for an eight-year-old (her parents are afraid that she might one day become the Prime Minister. They have very little understanding of politics and would rather see their daughter become a doctor – another profession they don't understand, but what the hell) and she will not allow you to treat her like a retard.

She asks intelligent questions that baffle your adult mind. Also, she has valid explanations for everything she does, including wearing pants and only pants, no skirts.

"It is wrong," she says, with a frown, "to show your legs."

It is both sad and surprising to hear that from someone whose legs are hardly long enough to merit concealment. You might argue with her that this is the only *age at which she might be allowed to show those spindly sticks anyway, but Divya has a ready argument to counter yours.*

Like most little girls, she imitates her mother and she has never seen her mother's legs. So there!

However, the matter does not rest there. The situation is a little more complex than might be settled through the invocation of her mother's legs. Divya's mother is a Bollywood fanatic and to make life easier for herself, she allows the children infinite freedom with the television.

Now, Divya is fiercely competitive and consequently, she has no friends at all. Her charming face and formidable linguistic abilities initially attract people but they soon begin to fear her and disappear. Somehow, this doesn't seem to bother Divya. She revels in the fact that she is always chosen to be the class monitor and is the star student of her tiny school. But since the television is always on, Divya has taught herself to study while watching movies.

And she has developed an unusual ambition. If asked why she is wasting her time on books if she is only interested in the movies, she will look sharply at you and say, "I want to study hard and become Karishma Kapoor."

Hmmm.

"And what about the legs?" you might ask. "You will have to show your legs to become a film actress."

At this, our little fighter will appear exasperated. "Don't you know it's all right for one to show one's legs in the movies?"

The movies, she will go on to explain, will be her job, which is really not what she represents. She is not her job. What she really 'is' has nothing to do with what she will do when you see her on the big screen.

And right there, you have your classical good-bad girl: the BIG.

A BIG knows her social milieu. She knows where and when to let herself fly. Her innocence – and you must believe in it – is intact while she dives into not-so-innocent waters. She will remind you that the person wearing the micro-mini is not her at all; that person was a put-on persona. She will turn your questions back on you and make you feel guilty for ever having doubted her.

Is she not always wearing pants at home? Is she not wearing those micro-minis only out of necessity? Oh, how could you doubt her? Howhowhow? What a horribly bad person you are!

Of course, tongues will continue to wag but our proud, misunderstood BIG will march on, fighting these battles, keeping her balance, and hoping against hope that she will one day be understood and her inherent GIGness recognized.

Legs

Mary contemplated the length of her skirt. She had folded it twice at the waist and the hem now dangled roughly an inch and a half above her knees. She wished she had not scraped her knees so ungracefully during the games period. She sighed. But at least she had shaved her legs and could afford to give the skirt another fold. Two-and-a-half inches of thigh, that would look good.

She pursed her lips and with neat and delicate turns raised her skirt another good inch. Her socks were rolled down to her ankles and the laces on her sneakers were left fashionably untied.

"What do you think," she asked Nikhil, the seven-year-old boy she was walking home. "Do I have nice legs?"

Nikhil studied her legs carefully and nodded. "Nice enough," he said.

"Will your brother think I am sexy?"

"*I* think you are very, very sexy," Nikhil said.

Mary laughed and, taking the boy's cheeks in her palms, kissed him loudly on his lips. Nikhil beamed and turned a happy pink. He too was falling in love with her.

It had rained the night before and the morning was crisp and sweet. Everything was clean. Mary felt absolutely happy being alive. She even liked Nikhil who was mostly annoying and disobedient, but this morning, skipping beside her in his bright blue jacket and bright red shoes, he was adorable.

"You know Nikhil," she said, "you are going to be one handsome guy when you grow up. You have such nice, serious eyes. You look like a mathematician. I think mathematicians are sexy."

She laughed and clapped her hands as though to emphasize the point. Then she twirled on her heel.

Nikhil's tiny heart was beating with joy by the time they reached the curve that led to his house. Mary stopped suddenly. She ran her fingers through her hair, smoothed down her skirt and sucked in her stomach.

"Do you think I should undo another button?" she asked.

She was breathless with excitement. She knew Adithya would open the door. Nikhil's mother was away for two days and his father would be at work. She would ring the bell. Adithya would open the door. It would be perfect. She would tell him she was having a horrifying time trying to pass her mathematics exams and he would invite her in. They would discuss her weaknesses and he would generously offer to tutor her, and she would very reluctantly accept.

Adithya was getting a Masters in mathematics! How exciting. She had never heard of anyone get a Masters in maths. Not even in books and movies.

"Do you think I should take off my watch?" she asked Nikhil, but they were already at the doorstep and she had already pressed the doorbell. She had no time to remove that gruesome watch; it was too black and did not match the colour of the skirt or the shirt. She wished she had worn a black skirt and not this godawful blue one.

Before she could moisten her lips with another dab of her chapstick, Adithya was at the door. He was casual in his white T-shirt, jeans and slippers. That haircut made him even more handsome and his eyes, like Nikhil's, were so brown and serious.

Mary swallowed and could not smile, nor could she tell him about her mathematical problems. She could hardly move and was piqued that Nikhil had let go of her hand so abruptly and run so quickly to his brother.

"Don't you think she is fuckin' sexy, Adi?" Nikhil asked, blushing pink and nuzzling into his brother's arm.

Adhithya frowned at his brother and ruffled his hair.

"Where did you learn to speak like that, champ?" he asked. "These are bad words. No using them, okay?"

"No, they're not," Nikhil said. "Mary says fuck all the time and I think Mary is fuckin' sexy too." He blushed deeper, pleased at getting the chance to publicly praise Mary.

Adithya looked at Mary and the frown was not fond any more.

"Please use decent language in front of my brother," he said, his voice cold and businesslike.

And Mary became painfully aware of the length of her skirt. Two-and–a-half inches above her knees. Precisely two-and–a-half inches too short.

Being a girl is hard. Being a good girl is very hard. But being a bad girl can darn right break your back!

It takes more than just guts to be a Bad Indian girl (henceforth referred to as BIG). It takes a smooth and manoeuvering nature, a measure of craftiness. One has to be adventurous and smart. Mostly, one has to be willing to be caught being bad, willing to spend money on clothes that can be worn only in a very few, select places. It is easier to be a BIG if a girl is socially amoral, if she does not think that lying and cheating are sinful, and is quick to forgive herself.

A BIG's life can quickly become very traumatic if she is not careful; and it is tiresome, being careful all the time.

Love, Lies and Delinquency

Hi. My name is Silky. What can I say about GIGs? I might be the wrong person to ask. The only good thing I have done in my life is to take good care of Peggy.

You know that I got thrown out, right? Actually, I only had to leave the hostel, not the college. But I dropped the year entirely and decided to start college from scratch.

What happened was this: Papa sent me away to study – in a convent! – after Pinky-di's *tamasha*. It was a really strict hostel. Nuns all over the place. I hated it and I had only one real friend there, Padma.

She and I had the Teena connection. When she found out that Teena-di lived with our family in Delhi, she came to my dorm to talk. Within a few days, she had taken me under her wing. She was in the third year and was at least five years older than all the others. She had got married when she was still in second year but her husband decided she must return to college to finish her BA degree. He thought she would not be able to concentrate on her studies if she continued to live at home, so he sent her to the convent.

Padma is not your typical good girl. Everyone knew that she had cheated in her exams. She didn't even wear bangles or a *mangalsutra,* except when her husband came to visit. But I liked her. She has this way of looking at you, a little sideways and yet right into you. And she never gets shocked, no matter what you tell her.

The warden very strongly disapproved of us hanging out

because, Padma being a married woman and all, she had the power to 'corrupt my mind'. What did the poor warden know? Anyway I didn't care about her disapproval.

Padma and I went out together on Sundays. We'd go around to the mall or to the cinema. Sometimes, there would be cute boys hanging around and we'd get talking to them and they would buy us things to eat, or cuddly toys. It was a lot of fun. If they asked for our names, we would say: "Carmen" and "Maria".

Sometimes the boys would drop us back to the hostel. They wanted promises about meeting or our phone numbers. We never carried our own cell phones on these outings; we always pretended that we weren't allowed to keep cell phones in the convent or we said that our phones had been confiscated by the nuns for some infraction of the hostel rules. If the boys got too insistent we would give them the hostel phone number.

The thing was, Carmen was our warden's name and Maria was an old sick-room nurse. So when these boys would call and ask to speak to 'Carmen' (it was mostly 'Carmen' they wanted – Padma), the warden would come huffing and puffing all the way down to the dorm phone.

The boy in question would say, "Carmen?"

She would say, "Yes, this is Sister Carmen speaking. Who is calling, please?"

"Aditya." (Or Karan or Raju or Samar)

"Aditya? I can't seem to…?"

"We met yesterday, remember?"

"I'm sorry but I do not remember meeting Aditya yesterday."

"Don't do this, *yaar*. Come on. You owe me a chocolate fudge too, remember?"

"Young man! You probably have the wrong number."

"Heyyy! Okay, fine, you don't owe me anything. But don't be like this. Talk to me, honey."

"Young man, I don't know what you're up to but I am warning

you, if this continues, I will call the police. This is completely inappropriate. Do you realize this is a convent? You want to do *badmaashi*? I will teach you a lesson you will not forget!"

And so on and on she would go, until the poor guy hung up, bewildered, or until Sister Carmen banged the phone down. Until next Sunday, when we went out again and found more admirers.

Once, a boy called Chintu called for 'Maria'. The old nurse went to the dorm phone. She was quite annoyed because she had already gotten out of her habit and had to rush out in a nightdress with only a scarf covering her bald head.

"Hello, is that you, Maria?" said Chintu.

"Yes it is."

"What happened to your voice, Maria? Are you alright?"

"I had a cold last week. Who is speaking?"

"It's me. Chintan, *yaar*. Chintu. Don't you recognize my voice?"

"I am afraid I don't, child. What do you want?"

"I just want to talk to you. So, how's Carmen doing?"

"She's well, praise the Lord. How do you know Sister Carmen?"

"I met her with you only, where else? At the movie."

A little gasp and snort followed.

"Child, I do not go to the movies. And, praise the Lord, neither does Carmen."

"Hahahaha! Good one. So what do you do in your free time, Maria?"

"I pray, child."

"Hahahahahaaaaa! Nice one."

Chintu was probably wiping his eyes, thinking of me and Padma in tank tops and tight jeans, movie tickets clutched in our hands, kneeling at the altar and praying for our souls.

"So," Chintan went on. "What do you wear when you go to bed, Maria? What are you wearing right now?"

Sister Maria, at this point, spluttered and choked, spluttered some more and banged the phone down.

There must have been many more such calls and eventually, they figured it out. It was rumoured that the nuns had a major private meeting. Afterwards, they called a hostel meeting and gave us long lectures on how good girls should behave and how they thought it was disgraceful, the way boys had started to call the hostel. Most disturbing of all, the girls were using the Sisters' names. Had we no shame left?

Padma and I never had much shame to begin with. We decided to be careful and yet, we couldn't resist doing it one last time. We did the whole name-giving charade again. The phone call happened, again.

Sister Carmen had wisened up. She had a long conversation with the boy who called. She tricked him into describing both of us, and questioned some of the other hostelites. Then we were called into her office for questioning. Padma didn't even bother to deny anything.

It was messy. Our families were called, our characters discussed. Our upbringing too. Papa wept, sitting there in Sister Carmen's office. Mummy had refused to come along with him. I too began to cry when I saw Papa crying.

Padma's husband was there. He just sat and listened, stone-faced, as Sister Carmen complained of our 'delinquency'. Then he asked Padma to go to her dorm and pack.

It has been almost a year since. Things are quiet at home. I've started English Honours at Delhi University. Overall, things are back to normal.

Padma and I still keep in touch. Sometimes, when she calls me, Papa picks up the phone. And she says, "Hello, this is Carmen speaking. Is your daughter well, Mr Singh?"

Being a good girl is not, usually, a choice. You could argue that not choosing is also a choice, but the repercussions of not being good are often so very bad that the choice of staying this side of GIGdom is a foregone conclusion. On the other hand, BIGdom is a matter of conscious choice and it entails the taking of a huge, huge risk.

The first thing you must understand about BIGdom is that a successful bad girl is an equally successful good girl. If her mother and father, brothers, sisters, the entire extended army of relatives have faith in her goodness, it is easy to step out of the house/neighbourhood/city/state/nation, and explore the temptation of being un-good. In fact, cloaked in the armour of other people's belief in her goodness, she might even get away with being bad inside her own house!

BIG Girls

The Singh household was, these days, rather precariously balanced on its head.

With six females in it, patriarch PP Singh had been feeling for a while that it was losing its male essence. For that is what it was: an essence. A house could be filled with a dozen women but if one man ruled over them all like a dark lord, frightening even at his most benign, the household would still smell male. There would be a faint odour of *man* coming off the furniture, the curtains, even the kitchen. Even the women. Like in his own childhood, all the women in the house had vaguely given off a 'man' essence. It was not a scent. Just a flavour.

Patriarch PP Singh had worked hard to recreate that flavour in his own family. The disappointment of not having sons had long since evaporated. And to tell the truth, he wasn't even sure he wanted sons. Sons are trouble. If he had a teenage son now, he'd be creating a little scene everyday – today a motorcycle; tomorrow a car; then girl-trouble, or he'd be out all night, smoking and drinking. Maybe there would be police trouble.

Now look at all those boys arrested near Rakabganj. Just think. They don't even leave the gurudwara alone. Forty of them, sitting in jail, having their bottoms reddened. Serves the monkeys right. But just think of their fathers. The police calling up in the middle of the night: 'Your son is in jail'. Going to the thana, paying money, doing *ji-huzoori*, licking the fat *thanedar's* arse.

Na ji, na. Daughters were just fine. And fine daughters they were too. They had not given him one day of trouble so far. All that shit other people said – daughters are hard to manage; daughters need to be watched and god knows what else. *He* never had to. People just did not know how to bring up girls. Now, his Mrs… she had needed a little managing. Not much. A few whacks now and then. But over the last five years, her will had settled into his so completely, it was hard to get her up to any decision at all. Even to go shopping at Diwali, she would just grunt at him, which could be interpreted any way he chose.

His three daughters, Gitoo, Pinky and Silky, were big girls now and they knew just what to do and what not to do. Gitoo was twenty-two, Pinky twenty and Silky nearly sixteen. But none of them asked for anything except money to go to college and a few nice clothes. These were all very reasonable demands and PP Singh was not an unreasonable man. Gitoo wasn't top of her class but she was manageable. Next year she would either clear the MBA entrance or she would be married. For Pinky and Silky, there was time.

But even since this new girl had entered the household, PP Singh had begun to feel as if the reins were no longer so firmly in his own hands. Not that she was any trouble. She was quieter than his wife, if that was possible for anyone but the deaf and dumb, and more nervous in his presence than all the rest put together.

Yet, his own pervasive essence had shrunk a little. With Teena in the house, it seemed as if the other side of the gender scale had grown heavier, as if the house had been tipped on its side.

For one, he no longer felt free to walk into any room he liked. Teena was his best friend's daughter and she herself had asked if she could come and stay. She had taken admission in a diploma course in Delhi and had made a phone call to the Singh household before she moved. All she had needed to say was: "Uncle, I need your protection."

PP Singh took her into the household in a heartbeat. A young girl in a new city, far away from her own family – though he had to confess to himself that he did not see why a young girl should leave her own home and move to a new city – should not remain without protection. *Na ji na,* he would not let her languish in hostels or paying guest accommodation.

All the same, she was twenty one years old – a young woman of marriageable age and not a member of his own family. So for the first time in his life, PP Singh was knocking on doors in his own house.

That in itself wasn't so bad. What had really turned the household on its head had been the little rebellion about the dog.

Patriarch PP Singh had employed a watchman for years but the man was getting old and it was hard to get trustworthy servants these days. So he decided to get a dog instead. So many thefts and robberies and murders these days. One needed a good guard dog.

Through a happy coincidence, the neighbours revealed that they knew somebody whose dog had just had a litter. An Alsatian. At this point, the patriarch made one little mistake. He asked for the dog in the presence of his girls.

The youngest, Silky, piped up at once, saying she wanted a girl dog.

The neighbours had laughed. PP Singh had smiled but firmly said, no. It would be a dog, not a bitch. Then Silky, for the first time in her short life, had taken a deep breath and talked back to her father.

"Then you only take care of it, Papa. We are all girls and we don't want to look after a boy dog."

The neighbours had laughed uproariously. Mr Kapoor had suggested that he give in right away; there wasn't a chance in hell that PP – whom many of his friends affectionately referred to as 'Patiala Peg' Singh – would ever wake up early to take the dog out for walks, or clean the dog's piss or shit. If the girls were going to get stuck with caring for the animal, they should get their way. Mrs Kapoor had simpered and suggested that a bitch would be far less trouble than young daughters at any rate.

His own wife had politely laughed along, but the four girls – Teena included – had flinched at the insult. As they stood there, unsmiling, PP Singh gave in and allowed a bitch into the house.

Peggy, they called her. It was his own wife's decision and he never understood why. What sort of name was Peggy? In fact, as their affection for the little she-pup grew, he noticed that the women of the household would call her anything they pleased. Sometimes, they called her Patti. Sometimes Peggy. Sometimes, it was just Puppy.

He didn't care much either way. The pup didn't care much for him either. She never came to him when he whistled, though he did notice that the bitch came running whenever the phone rang and she barked furiously until you finished the conversation.

Now, the patriarch was a heavy sleeper – his nightly dose of two Patiala pegs helped – and he knew that the bitch was a good guard. She 'grrrr'ed steadily at any approaching footstep. Not at the girls, but at everybody else including the watchman, the maid, and the man of the house himself. When the bitch barked at him for the first time, he had ordered that she be put outside, to sleep with the watchman in a cramped hut near the gates. This time, Pinky put her foot down.

"Peggy is a girl dog, Papa. She cannot sleep with a man. It isn't proper."

The prim tone of her voice and the moral assurance with which she bit her lips stopped her father from arguing further. How could he possibly say that it was alright for a girl of this household to sleep with a man?

Nevertheless, with a dog – even if it was a girl dog – in the house, PP Singh slept in peace.

Mrs Singh, on the other hand, was sleeping lighter and lighter these days. As it is, she hadn't been sleeping well for years, and what with her husband's Patiala peg-amplified snoring, and now this bitch's low, periodic 'grrr'ing, she woke up frequently.

Besides, her husband had begun to ask her to go to the girls' room at night – he used to check on the children himself at least once a night until Teena moved in – and she would get up to check three or four times.

If she could not sleep, she would go into the spare room, where the girls would sit up late studying when they had tests coming up. Here she would pace, waiting for morning, or she would sit down with one of their books, flipping through the pages. Teena was the only one who read any books outside of her syllabus texts, she realized.

The ash was the first clue. If Mrs Singh had had a stronger nose, she would have caught the stink first, but it wasn't until she saw the ash that she sniffed a bit harder and caught a whiff. Tobacco.

It was strange, discovering that smell all over again. The last time she remembered smelling it was inside her own house, before she got married. Her younger brother used to sneak in a cigarette or two when he thought he could get away with it. To this new smell, in her marital home, her first reaction was terror. For a few moments, she just stood there, staring at the carpet. It was a beige Kashmiri carpet, with a lot of intricate black and pale blue patterns woven through. You could easily miss ash on this sort of carpet. Was she imagining it?

But no, the smell was there. She knelt down on the carpet to confirm, just in case, before confronting anyone. She peered close. Ash it was, and it wasn't ordinary ash – it was a neat inch-long cylinder of ash that left absolutely zero room for doubt. Cigarette ash.

To her own great surprise, Mrs Singh brought her palm down on the intact, fragile cylinder and swept the evidence, quite literally, under the carpet. Her husband, for the first time in twenty three years, was not told about a matter of great import. The household was, indeed, standing with its heels in the air.

But the patriarch slept soundly and his Mrs thought it was best not to disturb his peace of mind. She decided to have the spare room aired more often and she took to brushing the Kashmiri carpet herself, telling the maid that it cost more than her own wedding dress, and it had better stay tip-top until Silky's wedding.

The second clue was tiny and plastic: embedded in a socket in their crowded bedroom, was the clip that went ahead of a wire of the type that usually led to a telephone. There was something exactly like that in the drawing room, which was actually connected to a telephone. Gitoo, Pinky and Teena already had mobile phones, of course, and Silky had been promised one later that month, as a birthday present. Mrs Singh did not say anything but couldn't help glancing at that corner of the wall each time she passed it.

One night, Mrs Singh thought she heard a very faint 'hello?' whispered somewhere in the dark house. She creaked upright and padded out of the room. Peggy-Patti-Puppy grrred in warning. There was absolute silence. Mrs Singh tiptoed up to the girls' bedroom and listened at the door. Silence.

She opened the door as noiselessly as she could, and looked inside. The room was dark and four shapes were huddled on two double beds that pretty much took up all the space in the room. She took two steps further in and nearly tripped over something that felt like a wire. She stepped over it carefully and went closer to the beds.

For a moment she stood there, looking at the girls' sleeping forms. In the dark, she bent over the jumbled plaits and patted one of the heads, not sure whose it was, and she left the room without switching on the lights.

The damning evidence showed up to ring the doorbell one afternoon. It was a courier, delivering a telephone bill from a private company. Their own landline phone used the government service. Mrs Singh glanced at the name on the envelope. The bill was in Gitanjali Singh's name and the alternative contact number given out was that of Gitoo's cell phone.

She quietly told the courier, "There's some mistake. The address is right but we do not use any such telephone service."

She slammed the door shut, struggling with her ragged breath. Five minutes later, when the doorbell rang again, she rushed to the bathroom and locked herself in. Silky was at home and her mother heard her answer the door. The courier's voice drifted in: "Madam, this should be delivered here. I checked, the address is this house."

That was the month Silky got her own cell phone. Mr PP Singh had been exceptionally generous. The phone came with five spare bodies – all bright colours, which she loved. Pinky sulked, saying that Papa loved Silky more. Their father laughed and said the youngest child always got the most, but why, what did Pinky want?

Promptly Pinky said: "A new belt. Silver. It is the latest fashion." And Gitoo said: "Then I also want a belt. I want a coppery-gold colour." Silky protested: "It is my birthday. Why is everyone else getting new things?"

Mrs Singh quietly watched her daughters banter with their father. Her gaze came to rest on Teena's quiet, caramel eyes. And she said: "If everyone is getting something, then Teena should too. Is she less than a daughter to us?"

The patriarch rushed to agree with her but all his sentences seemed to come out jumbled and it took him a long time to say that today everybody would get what they wanted, and why didn't they all go shopping with their mother?

So they went shopping in a large, new mall. Mrs Singh plodded along heavily behind the spry girls, their long, silken hair hanging loose against their firm hips. She found a chair and sat down to watch them riffle through the racks. They seemed to want mostly party tops and party bags and belts.

On the way back, in a tired monotone, she asked: "Where will you wear all this? It is just a waste of money, isn't it?"

The question wasn't directed at any one of the girls. The silence lasted only a fraction of a second. Gitoo said: "So what, Mummy? Papa has the money. We can wear all this inside the house only."

Mrs Singh's gaze fell on Teena again, who was smiling distractedly, looking out of the window.

That week, Mrs Singh hardly slept at all. The bitch had got used to her barefoot wanderings about the house at night and did not grrrr as she stepped out of her bedroom. She did not even protest as the mother bent down to pat her.

On Friday night, she stepped into the spare room, found it smelling of tobacco and decided to air it right away. She opened the window. The night smelt clean and fresh. It was late August and the rains had left the city tender and fragrant. She leaned out of the window, looked at the moon, the hushed houses, the glint of metal outside their house.

The glint of metal outside? She squinted in its direction. It was a car.

Reluctantly, she turned her head to the left, towards the girls' bedroom window, which did not open out to the front of the house but along the side, directly opening into a side lane. There was a snake-like thing emerging from it, running all the way down to the road below. It was a rope ladder.

Mrs Singh turned to look at the car again. It was parked discreetly, under a tree, behind a stretch of wildly overgrown honeysuckle in the neighbour's garden. She quietly closed the window and went to the girls' room. The bitch was sitting guard outside and let out a rather loud grrrr.

By the time Mrs Singh entered the room, she found four huddled shapes in bed, the covers drawn up over their heads. She went back to her own bed and lay down. At five in the morning, she padded into the girls' bedroom again. Four huddled shapes and jumbled plaits. Fast asleep. Carefully, she retreated, keeping an eye out for telephone wires.

Teena was almost falling into her cornflakes the next morning.

Mr PP asked: "What's the matter? Didn't you sleep well at night?"

The girl glanced briefly at the other three before replying. "No, uncle. This Pinky kept talking half the night."

Pinky's father promptly launched into a lecture about the benefits of restful, unbroken sleep and the need for discipline in one's life. A routine was necessary. Even for sleeping and eating. They didn't realize it now but they would in ten years' time. And so on.

Mrs Singh looked at Teena's exhausted face and fought down a wave of annoyance.

On Sunday, the girls wanted to go and see a movie. The patriarch forked out the money but Mrs Singh snapped something about being too old to play *ayah* to such grown-up girls. Mr PP looked bewildered. The house was not only standing on its head, but clearly, it was wearing a skirt instead of pants. Anyhow, he agreed to take the girls out in her stead. He even put on a crisp new kurta, since Gitoo insisted she wouldn't be seen outdoors with a shabby man.

In the sudden emptiness of the house, Mrs Singh walked through the rooms feeling weightless. Usually, the girls kept their cupboards locked during the day. They had started the locking-up business last year, after one of her girls tried to wear the other's clothes to college. Mrs Singh didn't remember who started it but it turned into a very loud fight at the dinner table, which her husband had broken up by threatening to smack the next talking mouth. Since that day, all of them, except Teena, kept their cupboards locked. Besides, they told their mother, it was safer: the maid went into the room twice a day and… who knew?

Today, the girls had left in a hurry. All the cupboards were unlocked. Mrs Singh opened the cupboards one by one. In Gitoo's cupboard, she found the landline telephone, a pack of cigarettes, one whole shelf crammed with transparent, glitzy party clothes. In Pinky's, she found valentine's day cards and friendship cards and cuddly teddy bears holding velvet hearts. The cards were signed by two different names in two different handwritings, both dated the same year. In Silky's cupboard, she found backdated issues of *Penthouse*.

She knew already what she would find in Teena's: the diary, which she had found the first time she looked in the girl's cupboard. She had already taken the liberty of dipping into it.

Mrs Singh locked and chained the main door. She poured herself a Patiala peg from her husband's mini-bar, extracted a cigarette from Gitoo's pack and lit it using the kitchen stove. She picked up Teena's diary and went to sit in the spare room, oblivious to the bitch's puzzled grrring at so much unusual activity in the middle of the warm afternoon. She settled down on the Kashmiri carpet, took a long puff, and patted the space near her feet.

"PP!" she cooed. "PP… Come PP, come! Sit!"

Everyone has an opinion on the subject of GIGs but very few people agree to be pinned down to their views on BIGs. But a curious insight into how people judge a modern Indian girl's moral values came from a chance conversation with a professor of Punjabi literature in Chandigarh.

Conversation had somehow drifted towards girls and their security on campus. This gentleman, who had been chewing his moustache patiently for several minutes, finally spoke up: "These days, girls are not like that."

Like what, we asked.

He slowly warmed to his theme and got more and more agitated with each sentence.

"Like they used to be. The other day, one of my students admitted that she carried three different mobile phones. She showed me. All different models, different numbers. One was gifted by her parents. Two were gifts from boys. She never gives the same number to more than one boy. It means she is two-timing at least three boys. Who knows how many others? The girls nowadays... you should see them. They're half undressed. Naturally, boys get provoked. Girls stand around on the street, walk in markets, talk openly to boys. They go around on bikes and scooters. In this city, the girls are too bold. You get on a bus, especially night buses that go up to the hills, and you see these students – girls and boys huddled close, even holding hands. It was unthinkable in our time... well, times have changed. And what is the meaning of carrying so many mobile phones? Which good girl needs more than one phone, you tell me – what type of girl?"

Good Boys

Hi. This is Teena again. Whatever you've heard about the Singh girls, I just want to tell you they are nice girls. A little wild but basically good girls. And the boys they went out with (good god, they bored me no end) were nice boys. They were decent.

I don't know how to explain it but when you looked at them, you didn't feel like it was such a shocking thing to go out with them even if you were climbing out of bedroom windows at midnight. I mean, they had cars. They had money so we didn't go to seedy places. Only to the best clubs, where there was a good crowd. Decent people, you know?

It was Gitoo who started it all. She wanted to go out with this guy but of course, she wouldn't go out alone with him. This was Delhi and none of us went out alone in a car with a guy, no matter whether it was day or night.

So Gitoo started making plans. She got a different landline connection because the girls wanted to talk to boys. They were afraid Singh Uncle might glance at their phones and a name might pop up and unpleasant questions would be asked. Also, there was a complex moral negotiation involved. See, everyone gives out cell phone numbers these days, and hardly anyone gives landline numbers. It is normal, especially for girls who do not want the family to answer the phone when the boys call. But Gitoo had worked out that if boys found out you were lying to your own family, or going out without your father's permission, then their respect for you went down a little bit. Gitoo used to insist that it was very important for a guy to realize that he was not more important to you than your own father. So she would insist on giving a landline number. This would create an impression that the Singh sisters were not crossing any lines as far as their father's authority was concerned.

Whenever the Singh sisters found a boy one of them liked, they would get his number and ask him to wait until they called. They would plug in the phone only at night, so that even if the guy had caller-ID, there was no risk of getting calls from strangers during the day, when we were in our classrooms.

Then one day Gitoo bought the rope ladder. She actually sold one of her gold chains to buy it – you wouldn't believe how expensive a good, thick rope ladder can be. She said it was a worthwhile investment. Going to clubs cost so much more. I tried to stay back but I was out-voted. Gitoo wanted to take me along and Pinky was adamant that she would go too, which meant we couldn't possibly not take Silky. So we all went.

My heart was in my mouth all through. I kept thinking that Singh Uncle would hold me responsible. I don't know why *I* felt so guilty when it was the Singh sisters who wanted to go out. But I was terrified that if Singh Uncle found out, he would throw me out and I would have to go back to my ancestral house, where my Chacha-ji lived.

At first, there was just Gitoo's boyfriend. But since there were three unescorted girls, other boys began to show up. Silky, fast little thing, promptly latched on to an eighteen-year-old sardar boy. We were all very disapproving since she was still a school-kid. But it turned out fine because the sardar never tried anything funny. Perhaps because we were there to keep an eye.

Pinky hung around with this nineteen-year-old Muslim boy – very quiet and very drunk. It was a default sort of pairing. He wanted to be out partying in decent clubs but you needed a girl to get in. So he asked Gitoo if he could tag along as Pinky's date. Once inside the club, he didn't even try to hold her hand.

Silky was the one who enjoyed our nightly adventures. She danced a lot and she danced dirty. But she didn't dare try the booze with us older girls looking on, though I suspect she wanted to. She had been reading too many Jackie Collins books that year.

She's quite something, you know. She was the baby of the household, but it was she who went out and got her own cell phone. Singh Uncle didn't even know. She just begged for extra pocket money, then kept dipping into Singh Aunty's purse while she napped in the afternoons. That didn't stop her from harassing her dad about buying her another cell phone, of course. She kept pestering him, complaining loudly that both her elder sisters had phones and she needed one too. So finally he bought her a nice phone. It was quite funny afterwards, watching her scrabbling in her bag, squinting at each phone to see which one was ringing.

They tried to get one more boy along, anxious that I get paired up with someone. One night a boy came, riding a motorbike – tall and only seventeen years old. I rolled my eyes and didn't even say 'hello' properly. He didn't show up again and the boys gave up on me as a lost cause.

Gitoo was seeing this guy who was twenty-five years old. He was a young man, really, not a boy. He had a job and he lived in a flat. He was clearly in for something more than just drinks and dancing. But Gitoo was nobody's donkey. She refused to meet him in his house and when she did go out with him, it was always in a group.

Our Gitoo is not the type to give it up so easily. She strung him along, waiting to see if he could wait. She thought he might be a good marriage prospect but she wanted to check if he was the staying type.

There were two cars, always. Gitoo's fellow tried to manipulate it in such a way that we girls would be dumped in the other car along with the Muslim boy and the sardar, while he could take Gitoo alone in his own car. But Gitoo was always one step ahead of him. She would very sweetly link her arm in mine and gently pull me along, whispering into my ears and giggling at complete gibberish – it was all one big *sho-sha*. Then she would make me sit up front, in the seat beside her boyfriend, while she herself sat at the back, an elbow resting on each of our shoulders. Every so often, she'd lean forward to switch between FM stations. If she found a peppy number, she would jog her shoulders happily, her bright, excited eyes looking out at the dark road.

The Singh sisters loved the dark. I saw the look in their eyes when they were out at night, even if it was just with their parents, going to a late movie show. The lonely, lovely Delhi roads. The faint smell of ash and rot coming off the garbage dumps. The music and dance. Those girls were mad about music and dance.

And the boys were finally decent boys. So, even though I was terrified that we would be found out, even though I knew I was finished if Singh Uncle threw me out of his house, I went along.

I'm pretty sure Aunty knew. I mean, the way she looked at us after one of our nights out. I noticed how often the room was being aired, the one with the Kashmiri carpet. But she didn't say anything so maybe she didn't mind. Maybe she was even more afraid of what Uncle would do if he found out, so she kept our secret.

Gitoo went on to do her MBA and three years later, she got married to that same twenty-five-year-old. He was twenty-eight by then, making pots of money in a firm specializing in corporate law. He was Hindu and there were some fireworks when Singh Uncle found out, but Gitoo managed everything to her advantage.

Apparently, Uncle was convinced that the boyfriend was 'genuine' and therefore a decent match for his eldest. This conviction came about when his future son-in-law pulled up at the door in a shiny, black Mercedes and a bunch of violently blue flowers of which none of them knew the name.

As for Silky, she is learning belly dancing – her father didn't raise any objections when he found out it was an all-girls' class – and shows no desire to go out clubbing. She still reads Jackie Collins but she has begun to dip into Maupassant and Lessing too. Who would have thought, eh?

Like we mentioned, good is not the opposite of bad. It is just a condition that people find convenient, one which they attempt to perpetuate through a complex system of approval and disapproval. A Good Indian Girl bows to this system further than the rest, that's all.

How does she do this?

Above all, she remembers what not to do, and where. That is what 'saleeqa' *is. That is* 'tameez'. *To know how to behave and in front of whom. For instance, in most parts of India, GIGs are defined as those who do not smoke, do not drink, do not have boyfriends, do not have premarital sex and do not wear western clothes – give or take a few subjective add-ons.*

But in the average boarding school in Dehradun much of the above was tolerated. For instance, the students tolerated:

- *Girls smoking*
- *Girls drinking*
- *Girls using bad language*
- *Girls with a repertoire of dirty jokes*
- *Girls sleeping together*
- *Girls bathing together*
- *Girls who claimed to love girls*
- *Girls who fought like cats… with girls, and with boys*
- *Girls who never got decent grades*
- *Girls who were disrespectful to their elders*
- *Girls who were mean and rejoiced at somebody else's death*
- *Girls who stole*

The one thing they did NOT tolerate was 'unfaithful girls'. You did not stop being somebody's girlfriend for no good reason. It just Wasn't Done.

Satyagrah

Pinky awoke fairly late to a love that, she was certain, had been there all along. Suppressed all this while by her overwhelming sense of duty to her parents and responsibility to her sisters, she said, this love would no longer behave itself in the living grave of her heart, despite her best efforts. It was love, she said, that was driving her up the wall, not letting her sleep or eat. Or bathe.

Indeed. Pinky hadn't had a bath for nearly eight days now. Now our Pinky, she has always been a naturally indolent sort: she wouldn't stretch her arm out to unhook a fork from the cutlery stand on the breakfast table; she would instead poke at her bowl of mangoes or lychees with a fingernail until Mrs Singh or one of her sisters shoved a fork into her hand, usually with the phrase: "Don't be disgusting!"

On the best of days, she was the last person in the house to take a bath. Which suited everyone just fine because after she took a bath, she never bothered to wipe the bathroom floor dry or even switch off the lights and geyser. In winter, it was generally accepted that Pinky would take a bath only on alternate days and even then, Mrs Singh had to remember to switch on the geyser half an hour before, hang up the towel and goad her second daughter towards the bathroom with little threats that escalated from the whipping of her bony bottom to a ritual skinning in boiling water.

So Pinky not taking a bath for a day or two wouldn't have been noticed even in her own house. Since she did nothing, she didn't sweat much, even in the summer, three whole days and two nights passed before Mrs Singh noticed the tangles in her daughter's hair and asked why she hadn't brushed her hair. Pinky glared at her silently and stalked off into her own room.

This stalking off was a bit of an event. Pinky never, *ever*, stalked. It just wasn't in her personality. She would burst into tears. She would sulk. She would refuse to use forks and spoons on the dining table. But getting up and stamping her little feet to show her displeasure was far too energetic; it just wasn't her style. So this time, even her father looked up from his second Patiala peg of the evening, and wondered aloud if something was wrong with our Pinky.

Mrs Singh was getting a bit indolent herself in her middle age. So she didn't bother to ask any more questions until the next morning, when it became clear that not only had our Pinky not been bathing but she had also decided not to brush her hair. Or her teeth.

Now, our Pinky possesses – as you will soon find out – a capacity for sustained non-violent *satyagrah*. However, hunger strikes were beyond her. If anything, she ate more than ever and her bottom had stopped being bony a few years ago. She ate constantly. Almonds. Namkeen. Bhajia. Sandwiches. Butter on Monaco biscuits. Jam on Marie biscuits. And all her meals. Unbathed, unbrushed, she ate.

On the morning of the fourth day, her mouth told its own tale of distress in a fairly loud way, bringing the family's attention to the long-buried ache of Pinky's heart. So, at the breakfast table, Mrs Singh had felt obliged to ask at last.

"What is wrong with you?"

Pinky sighed deeply and, rather dramatically, unleashed a long, indolent stream of silent tears. The household was aghast. What's wrong? What's the matter? What's happened?

And that was how Pinky announced that she was in love.

Now, Mr PP Singh was not an unreasonable man. He had witnessed and survived his oldest daughter's revelation of romance a year ago, and had even showed a great deal of forbearance when the lover turned up at home to ask for her hand. He would have felt perfectly justified in giving the young man a few hard smacks before he finally agreed to the match. But he had desisted. The times were changing. And a man who had three daughters had better change with the times.

But now that Pinky was recreating some romantic drama, the patriarch felt more than equal to the situation. He had experience. He drew in a visibly sharp breath, set his hard belly against the edge of the breakfast table and grunted. This was a signal to indicate that he wasn't happy at all, but he was listening.

Pinky had practiced this for a while. She had, in fact, practiced too hard. Her hiccups and her rapidly receding tears were too aesthetic overall, though nobody except her mother seemed to notice. Mrs Singh was itching to let the girl have a few tight slaps; that would do her good, as would a cold shower. But she was curious too, so she waited.

"I love him," Pinky was saying.

Mr PP grunted again. Even the youngest sister, Silky, was looking interested now; this was an unexpected development. Pinky and *love*? Everybody knew she was too lazy to undertake anything serious.

"I didn't say anything all this time because I love you. All of you. My family..."

A fresh stream of tears, a sob and a hiccup before she went on. "I thought, what will happen if people find out? What will they say about you, and what about Silky, who will marry her if people begin to talk like this about me?"

Silky cut in. "You don't need to worry about me." She stole a look at her father's purple face and added, "I am not even interested in marriage. I'll stay with Papa."

Pinky would have rolled her reddening eyes, but this would have spoilt her performance and distracted everyone from the agenda. She simply sniffled.

Mrs Singh prodded, "So this had been going on from… before Gitoo's wedding?"

Pinky hiccupped in response.

"Since when?"

"A long time. Since Gitoo knew her boy."

Mrs Singh was starting to get a little alarmed now. "And why didn't you tell us earlier?"

"Gitoo had to get married first. She was older."

Silky was getting impatient. "But who is this guy? What's his name?"

Pinky allowed herself two more hiccups before whispering: "Ali."

A dark, heavy, silence descended on the room. Mr PP Singh leaned back, then leaned forward and crossed and uncrossed his arms. Mrs Singh swallowed and looked stunned.

Silky drew in her breath sharply and widened her eyes. *Ali?* The quiet nineteen-year-old, who had looked like he'd been slapped if you batted your lashes at him? The boy who just sat there in the car looking miserable until he was inside the disco where he proceeded to drink himself silly? Gitoo used to say that their *Jija-ji* used to say that Ali was basically into drinking, not girls. His only true love was, and would be, the bottle.

Pinky hadn't shown much interest in him either. She used to flirt with him in a detached sort of way sometimes, just to embarrass him, but she would discard him as soon as they were inside the club and would start dancing with Teena or her sisters instead.

Silky was the first to speak. "Ali? You said *Ali?*"

"Ali. He's Muslim."

Having stated the obvious, Pinky shrank back into the sofa and didn't raise her eyes. She sniffled into her laced fingers and then began to speak in a rush.

"I knew him only through Gitoo. I swear. Gitoo used to go out to meet her boyfriend at night and she wanted someone to go with her. That's the only reason I went along, just to give her company, and then this boy was also there. He was *Jija-ji*'s friend. Gitoo used to get busy with *Jija-ji* and so, Ali and I just started to talk to each other, and then I started liking him because I found out he is a really nice person. Really, he is such a genuine boy, Papa."

Silky's heart was in her throat and beating so violently, she thought she would have a stroke. Any moment now, her idiot sister would spill the whole bag of beans. Knowing Pinky, she would too, just to make herself look better or at least, no worse than her sisters. After that convent mess last year, Silky didn't think her father would forgive any new revelation of her transgressions – rope ladders and bedroom windows, cavorting in discos... She was sure her father would skin her alive.

She glanced at him as he slowly leaned forward, gripping the edge of the table with his burly paws. Any moment now, she thought, he would pull himself up and off his chair, and whack Pinky. She hoped he would, but was also terrified that he would.

PP Singh only grunted. He did not get up.

"He is not a bad boy. No cigarette. No drinks," Pinky went on and on, oblivious to Silky's widening, warning eyes.

"And he is the only son. Papa, I love him, Papa."

Papa finally did haul himself up and strode across the room towards his cowering daughter. Mrs Singh, however, had risen already and was standing between them.

In a fierce whisper, she said, "*Na ji*. She is a grown-up girl. God knows what she might do."

Mr PP Singh, the patriarch, contented himself with pacing back and forth. Then he abruptly stopped and declared, "*Bas*. I no longer trust you. You are not going out of this house now."

Pinky whined, "But I will die without him."

This statement was met with an ominous silence, which suggested that nobody in this household would mourn her death.

Mr PP Singh strode out of the room. Silky muttered something about a history project and left the room.

Mrs Singh quietly said, "Enough. Go take a bath now."

Then she went to her husband's side to offer comfort and advice, and by turns, to gently rebuke him about how he had given the girls too much freedom, and look, this is how one's children repaid one's love.

Pinky had been fully prepared for a beating and was rather shocked that she had been spared one. She stood up, trembling despite herself, and rued the fact that she hadn't finished her cornflakes before having this conversation. She considered finishing breakfast, but decided that this might be a bit much. So she went back to her room and lay down. Which is what she did anyway on a daily basis, until it was time to have a bath.

Around noon, her mother stepped into her room, glared at her and said, "Go take a bath. Enough is enough."

Pinky sniffed and turned on her side, facing the wall. Mrs Singh contented herself with slapping her daughter on the bottom and mumbling obscenities under her breath as she walked away.

And so passed the fourth day. Pinky, while not saying another word on the subject of love or Ali, wasn't on a hunger strike. She would wait until the house grew absolutely still, tiptoe out to the kitchen, grab a slice of bread and some juice, or a paratha, and dash back to her room. Her mother would plod out when she heard the sound of the fridge opening and closing, and yell: "Pinky, take a bath, *khasmanukhani*!", or "Pinky, brush your teeth or I'll knock them all out", and even "*Khoti*, have you no shame?"

Any shame Pinky felt, she reserved for the onerous task of not taking a bath and not brushing her teeth and hair. This went on until the next morning. Mr PP Singh did not show up for breakfast. He was silently fuming and didn't trust himself not to beat the girl. His wife held him back, afraid that one really hard slap might break their daughter's neck or shatter her jaw: she herself had not forgotten the near-fatal impact of his blows when he was angry, in the first few turbulent years of their marriage. So she kept up a steady stream of chatter alternately advising restraint ("It is a delicate situation. We have to handle it delicately or it will slip out of our hands") and abusing the bitch she had brought up to be so shameless ("*Arre*, even that pup, Peggy, has more decency").

Peggy/Patti-the-bitch had indeed grown into a remarkably confident adult, but had shown no signs whatsoever of amorous anxiety, not even in heat.

Without a trace of shame, Pinky woke up the next morning and showed up for breakfast. She found the table had not been laid, and no mother stood in the kitchen preparing any food. So Pinky went straight to the kitchen to help herself to instant noodles and coffee. Silky emerged from the bedroom and joined her sister in the kitchen.

"Pinky-di, mad or what?" she hissed.

"Shut up." Pinky murmured back, quite calmly.

"Ali? You didn't even like him."

"I like him now. And you don't wag your tongue around too much or you'll be banned from leaving the house too."

"Like I care?" Silky shrugged, but her heart was beating fast. "*I* never did anything. I'll say you and Gitoo forced me to come with you. I was only a child then."

"Oh? And all that grinding? Rubbing hips with strangers on the dance floor? Having cell phones that boys give you, which Papa doesn't even know about? Who forced you to do that?"

Silky opened her mouth to say that she was certain Papa wouldn't believe such lies, but then, she shut her mouth again. Papa would believe it. Now, he would believe anything. The fact that her boy had been a sardar would not help much; she knew that Papa expected her to marry a sardar eventually, but he was also very suspicious of young sardar boys, especially the ones who went out late at night with girls in cars and got drunk.

Silky was in no mood to court house arrest, so she helped herself to a generous portion of the spicy noodles that Pinky had just finished making, suffered a protesting slap on the hand from her disgraced, eternally hungry sister, and stalked off to her room. She liked to eat in peace, in the loving company of the Internet.

Meanwhile, Pinky finished eating her noodles standing in a corner of the kitchen instead of sitting down at the dining table. Then she set about making toast and tea. She put it on a large tray along with the butter dish and a bottle of Kissan, which was the only jam her father would eat. And she carried the tray into her parents' bedroom.

The door, as usual, was wide open and she walked right in, eyes downcast. Nobody knocked on doors in the Singh household, unless there was a stranger in the house.

"Papa, Mummy. Eat a little."

Her voice was contrite, mellow, even a little fearful, and her parents were utterly flabbergasted. This, they hadn't expected. She allowed herself a quick glance at their expressions and set the tray down on the side table.

"Papa, Mummy, I don't like to see you so worried. If I have made a mistake, I should suffer. Why should you suffer? Please eat."

Mrs Singh knew the girl had already breakfasted and wasn't suffering in the least. She sighed.

"Pinky, have you brushed your teeth?" she asked, but her voice betrayed that she was quite without hope. The girl looked unbrushed and unwashed head-to-toe.

"Mummy," and her voice trembled a little. "Mummy, I cannot! I cannot live like this. And what is the use of bathing and brushing my teeth if I cannot live?"

"Oh, what a she-donkey! What a bitch I have birthed! The same old chant? You know it is not possible. Didn't you know that?"

"I knew, Mummy, I knew. That is why I didn't say anything all these years. And I know that anything I do will affect Silky's life too. As it is, after the convent thing, you are wondering – who will marry her? Nobody from a good family will marry her if I, if I…" and her voice faltered, shook and squeaked to a halt.

The patriarch, who had slept little and drunk a lot last night, found his bloodshot eyes suddenly full with tears.

"*Beta,* if you care so much about us, about your sister, then why are you doing this to us?"

"But Papa, what have I done?" and here she pinched the skin of her throat between her thumb and forefinger. "*Sau*… I have not *done* anything."

Her mother drew her breath in sharply. Mr PP Singh thought he was going to get an instantaneous attack of diarrhoea. They had only begun to grapple with the notion of a romantic linkage between their lazy, languid Pinky and some faceless, perhaps white skull-capped 'Ali'. The notion that they might have actually 'done' something had not yet presented itself to their minds.

Slowly Mrs Singh exhaled, licked her dry lips and sat down heavily on the bed.

"So… so, then, what do you want?"

Pinky rushed towards her and sat down near her feet.

"Mummy, get Silky married."

"What? Why?"

"I promise, I will not do anything," and at this point, she had the sense to lower her head and look ashamed during this fractional pause, "anything that you or Papa don't want me to do. Not until Silky gets married."

Mr PP Singh shook his head vigorously and put a heavy, firm hand on his daughter's head.

"*Oye vekh,* Pinky. Anything you said, we did for you. But this – no! Not now. Not after Silky is married. Never."

With the solid weight of his hand on her head, Pinky didn't dare shake her head or speak. Very carefully, she shifted herself out of his reach, stood up, sighed, and went to her own room.

Mrs Singh picked up a cup of tea, handed it to her husband and then took long, thoughtful sips from her own cup. She picked up a slice of toast, buttered it. Slowly, she chewed. This was going to be a long battle and both sides needed to conserve their energy, replenishing themselves often.

And so the fifth day passed like the fourth. Pinky's hair was matted like a street urchin's and even if circumstances had been less emotionally fraught, the likelihood of her family giving her a hug or kiss at this point was very remote. Even she was beginning to feel like a bath might be a good idea. The day was humid and her skin prickled around her back and down the insides of her legs. But she persevered.

All through the fifth day, she sat at a windowsill. Mr PP Singh rushed up several times, assuming she was sitting there because she was waiting for a signal from the street below.

He had been pacing the room in his vest and pyjamas, barefoot, with a revolver tucked into his pyjama cord and his long hair undone, hanging down his back in stringy wisps of grey-brown. But outside the window, there was no man. Not even a fellow-sardar. The summer street sat baking in silence all afternoon, until people started to open their windows and school buses growled up with loads of scamper and noise.

Silky made a face when she saw signs of her sister's sustained campaign. She said she would have to sleep outside the bedroom, on the sofa, if this went on, and how much longer would this *tamasha* go on?

Nobody answered her. Not even Peggy-Patti, who had been lying low, head between paws, for the last two days. Even she seemed to shrink a little and looked dazed when Pinky walked past.

On day six, Mrs Singh hit upon a solution. She cut off the air-conditioning in all rooms but her own. That *karamjali* second daughter of hers would have to obey and take a bath at least to cool off. The Muslim boy could be dealt with later.

The daughter was tempted to obey. When Pinky rubbed her neck, tiny rolls of black filth formed and stuck to her fingers. Her mouth felt sticky, her tongue felt – and actually, it was – coated with a thick film of yellow-white residue. Very slyly, having washed her hands after a meal – she ate a hearty five of them – she slipped a wet palm under her dress and ran it across her armpit. That brought an illusion of relief, for about half a minute. But she persevered. This couldn't go on forever, she told herself. Sooner or later, they'd give in.

On the morning of the seventh day, the patriarch showed signs of cracking. His eyes were bloodshot with exhaustion since he was sleeping very lightly, sitting up at the slightest noise, afraid that Pinky would run away at night. His shoulders hunched. Listlessly, he shuffled about.

Mrs Singh, on the other hand, had slept deep and woken refreshed. She knew that if running away had been on the agenda, the window and the rope ladder would have been used years before. Clearly, Pinky was angling for something else, not escape.

She also knew her daughter well enough to know that of all her girls, this was the one who cared least about family approval. If she really wanted to marry that boy, she would do so against their wishes. But what, then, did Pinky want? Why did she not just spell it out?

At any rate, Mrs Singh had air-conditioning on her side, so she conserved her energy and plotted. Her sole worry at the moment was that the girl would get lice in her nice long hair if she didn't wash it and brush it out soon. She might even get – shudder shudder – maybe even *body lice.*

That afternoon, Gitoo breezed into the house, eyes bright with an odd mixture of anger, fear and excitement. Silky had told her everything on the phone. Her first reaction was anger – it had been an unspoken agreement that none of the sisters would ever mention those secret outings, and Pinky had let the secret out.

Now, Gitoo was nervous. She knew that her being a married woman would not stop her Papa from giving her a thwack or two if he was really angry. At least, Silky hadn't been implicated yet, but their mother was sharp enough to find out once she started asking questions.

Gitoo knew she was going to get into very serious trouble with her mother. She could already hear the forthcoming accusations inside her head: "We trusted you and this is what we get?" "You were the eldest. This is what you taught your sisters?" "*Arre*, better you'd strangled her with your own hands than let it come to this."

Oh no, Gitoo didn't want to meet her family today. On the other hand, Ali? *That* Ali? Reedy, silent, so utterly besotted with the bottle? She had to get to the bottom of this.

In the drawing room, she found her Papa glowering, too exhausted to even shout at her effectively. Silky was busy with her computer, as usual. Pinky was curled up on her bed. Apple cores and chocolate wrappers littered the floor.

Gitoo went into her mother's bedroom, sweating already and reeling from the sight of her unwashed, unbrushed sister. Mrs Singh, instead of greeting her married daughter with the tight slap she was expecting, beckoned her inside, shut the door and asked her if she'd eaten lunch yet.

Gitoo nodded. Her mother got up, brought out an old Dalda can and set it on the bed on front of her. It turned out to contain homemade dry fruit *laddoos*.

"Eat."

Gitoo didn't dare protest, as she usually would have, about her weight and the amount of calories this stuff contained. She picked one up quietly and took a tiny bite, keeping her head bent low.

"So?" her mother said.

"Mummy..." Gitoo's mind seemed to have suddenly stopped working.

"*Haan.*"

"Mummy, I, I was… Mummy –"

"*Chhad!*"

"*Hain?*"

"Let it be. You are married. It is done. No point crying over it now."

Gitoo allowed herself a larger bite of the *laddoo*. Then another. And then she ate all of it. The situation called for calories. Finally, she found her voice.

"So, Mummy, now?"

"Do something," her mother ordered. "This is your doing only. Now you find out."

Off Gitoo went, reluctant to leave the air-conditioned room but duty bound. She sat at the foot of Pinky's bed and tickled the soles of her grimy feet with a fingernail. Pinky sat up with a yelp.

"*Chal utth, nautanki!* What's all this?" snapped Gitoo.

Pinky wrinkled her nose and settled back into her pillows. She sighed. Gitoo tickled her soles again.

"Stop, didi."

"Get up, bitch. We have all had enough of this drama. You get the whole household up on your head, and then you lie around, sighing. Not one dot of shame."

Pinky knew better than to take the 'I cannot live without him' line with her sisters. She just pouted. Silky had abandoned the computer to join her sisters, but she sat on her own bed.

"Spit it out, *kamini*. Remember, I know how to deal with you." Gitoo prodded Pinky's foot as if she was going to break it.

"Didi, what *yaar*? You did what you wanted, got married and left. Now you are bullying me when I want to live my life."

"Who has stopped you from living your life? Go to college if you like. Work if you like. Get married if you like. Where is the problem?"

"I don't want to get married."

"Don't. What is this *tamasha* about Ali?"

"Didi, I said I don't want to get married."

Gitoo open and shut her mouth a few times. The youngest exchanged perplexed glances with the eldest. The middle one, they had always assumed, would be the one who'd get married first, and with minimum fuss. She was lazy, unambitious, fond of going out, fond of food and pretty clothes, and she had never expressed any preference for any particular kind of man. They had all assumed that she would gracefully bow to Papa's wishes and go on to make a nice, rounded Punjabi wife in due course. Everybody would have been happy.

"Why?" Gitoo finally asked.

Pinky sighed again, though it was not the melodramatic sighing she had been practicing lately.

"There is somebody in my life."

Silky groaned. "Not again. Don't start again. You can't be serious about him."

"Not Ali."

Gitoo frowned. This was not making sense. In fact, it was starting to sound truly dangerous. If Ali was only a Trojan horse, what greater disaster lurked in the belly of her sister?

"Then who?"

Pinky took a deep breath and shut her eyes.

"Don't kill me," she said.

Gitoo clicked her tongue impatiently.

"What could be worse than a drunkard Muslim lover?"

"Pintoo."

There was an ensuing silence. Neither sister knew what to say. Silky recovered first.

"Pin – Pin – Pintoo? *That* Pintoo?"

Gitoo's eyes were round as coins. "Silky's Pintoo?"

Pinky hung her head. Gitoo shook hers. Silky shook her head as if to clear it. A moment later, she burst out laughing.

"Well! I mean... alright! Alright! He's not *my* Pintoo. I don't mind. Gitoo-di, she can have Pintoo if she wants him. I don't."

"But Pinky, he is younger!" Gitoo protested. "He's a *bachcha, yaar.*"

"He's not a child," she sniffed. "And he's very smart, okay?"

Silky couldn't hold back her giggles.

"Pintoo? Smart? *Arre,* just let it be. Pinky-di has always had a thing for younger men. Even that Ali was younger to her."

"Six months!" Pinky protested. "Six months' difference does not mean he was younger to me. And even Pintoo is only two years younger. In olden times when nobody kept birth records, who went to check if the girl was younger to the boy before falling in love?"

Gitoo shook her head disbelievingly. "Are you serious? *Pintoo*?"

Pinky scratched at her ankle tentatively. "I like him," she said.

"But what does he do?"

"Nothing," Pinky said, moving up to scratch her shoulder and then behind her ear.

"Nothing?"

"Nothing."

Silky butted in. "He never did anything. Dropped out of college in second year. Total *ganwaar.* On top of everything, he thinks he is one *gabru.*"

"I think he *is* handsome," Pinky said quite firmly, as if she would brook no argument on this issue, and went on to scratch behind her other ear before she moved to her hair.

"But Pinky, you don't work either. If he doesn't work and you don't work, how will it work? And stop scratching. It is disgusting."

"I don't know, didi. That's why I said, I don't want to get married yet. I'll sit at home quietly, with Peggy and Papa and Mummy, until... well, until something starts to work."

Pinky was still scratching her hair.

"*Chhee!* Stop, Pinky!" Gitoo cried out. "Have you got lice already? And what nonsense is this? Not brushing your teeth or hair?"

But that line of conversation was pointless, of course. Pinky did not bother to answer.

Silky said, "Pinky-di, if you liked Pintoo, why didn't you tell me?"

Pinky sniffed. "You were so mean to him. He's so *seedha* and so sweet. He used to come to me to complain about you. And then he took me out on his bike, one day, and then I started liking him."

The eldest and the youngest exchanged worried glances. This was serious. Much more serious than Ali, who had his father's property at least to fall back upon, and had no siblings to bark at him as he drank away his inheritance. Pintoo didn't have an inheritance and he wasn't likely to have much more than a motorbike for the next few years. Perhaps, he would never have more. You couldn't run a household without money.

Gitoo stood up abruptly and paced the room. If she had been wearing a vest and pyjamas, and if she could have grown a beard and put on twenty kilos, she would look exactly like PP the patriarch at this moment. Her two sisters noticed this, but were wise enough not to say it.

Just as abruptly, Gitoo turned and left the room without a word. Silky paused for about ten seconds and then ran out behind her to look at what was going to happen. But the eldest sister was back inside her mother's bedroom. The door was firmly shut.

Fifteen minutes later, Mrs Singh had marched out of her own room, marched into the girls' bedroom, and stood glaring at her second daughter, who was lying down, vigorously scratching both her calves with both sets of fingernails.

The next thing anyone remembered seeing was Mrs Singh standing beside the bed with an empty, upturned bucket in her hands and a blinking, gasping Pinky lying in a very wet bed.

Mrs Singh turned around and faced her husband who was standing at the door, open-mouthed, stunned at the simplicity of this solution.

"*Suniye ji*. Enough! We will settle this matter once and for all. Pinky is to be married right away."

"Of course. Of course, she must be," he said, a little dazed. "But who will marry this girl now, the way she is behaving? If she opens her mouth, our *izzat* will be just like the mattress on that bed."

"She can open her smelly mouth all she likes. We will find her a family who does not care who says what, or what she says."

The patriarch shuddered and almost collapsed, thinking about the weight of such a Herculean task. Did such a family exist in this country?

"But where will we find such a boy?" he wondered aloud.

"I know someone," Mrs Singh said, and stomped off to her own room.

"You do?" He was close at her heels.

"Yes. Remember the Singhs who live in number 346? B-Block?"

"The auto-repair-wale Singhs?"

"Yes. Them. Their son."

"But this girl is insisting on, on A .... that Muslim. If the Singhs find out, what face will we show?"

Mrs Singh made an impatient smacking sound with the palm against her thighs.

"Firstly, I will dunk this girl so many times in so many buckets of water, she will also remember who is her mother. And secondly, their younger son, Pintoo, is not such a prize. If they say four things, we will have eight things to say to them. Go and talk to his father and tell him that marriage will settle the boy. We'll help also in any way we can."

"But that boy does nothing. He's a college dropout."

"Is he a sardar or is he not? *Bas*! You want her to marry some Ali?"

And so, Mr PP Singh the patriarch found himself organizing a very quick wedding for his second daughter to a boy his wife had picked out for her. To everyone who attended the wedding, he said, "It is a good family, and what do college degrees matter? Real learning happens in real life. You wait and watch, my Pinky will bring him double-triple success."

One of the most punishing things about being a GIG is the constant awareness of Mummy-Papa and their awful faith that the fragile little baby doll to whom they've dedicated the best part of their youth wouldn't do anything bad. Couldn't, not if she tried.

But what if she does?

Doesn't that go to show that Mummy-Papa made a mistake – gave her too much or too little of some vital ingredient that keeps other good girls good? Is it not a sign that they have failed her? Why else would she fail them?

Mammas and Papas cannot bring themselves to forget that their girls are THEIR girls. Papas, perhaps, more than Mammas. They forget that the girls are people who have been dealing with the big, bad world for years now. That they have met others completely unlike Papa, and have learnt to love, and loathe, independently. When parents are faced with the truth about their daughters, their hearts break. If they are reminded over and over, their hearts break over and over.

And that is why a GIG starts to construct tender webs of deceit, fierce in the protection of her father's heart.

Daddy's Girls

Conversations of consequence between father and daughter took place nowadays while he cooked. It could also be argued that these were not conversations, that they were Shakespearean monologues where statements and ideas were hammered in by the father until truth gushed forth – a pattern that made Preeti wary of this newfound bonding.

Already, even as Manmohan asked his daughter how long he needed to cook the *raajma,* she was alert, waiting for the innocuous questions that sought to feel out her lies. They took long to come, the questions, sometimes as long as a few days. But they came.

"How many whistles for the *raajma* to cook, Preeti?" Manmohan asked.

"At least eight."

"Eight! That is too many. I have not cooked *raajma* before but even I can tell that with eight whistles, the beans will be *halwa.*"

Preeti shook her head. There was no point arguing. In fact, now that he had asked her opinion and completely overruled it, she almost hoped the beans would come out raw.

Of late, Preeti had begun to be amused by her father. All her life, she had been either afraid or angry about the authority he held over her life, but ever since she got married... no, not since then. Ever since her mother had died and Preeti had gotten pregnant, Manmohan had shown a new side. He was still authoritarian; things still had to be done exactly the way he wanted. But he was authoritative in a different way now, the way mothers are. Here he was, in the kitchen – a room he had never entered before – working with beans and onions and tomatoes.

She had once described him to her husband thus: "Picture an ant," she'd said. "A protruding belly above hair-thin legs and a round head, complete with alert antennae. And an unending hurry to get from point A to point B to point C to point D to point E."

Her husband Mahesh, a.k.a. Mac, had laughed. "That sounds like you," he'd said.

It was true. Preeti was a lot like her father, especially now with a nine-month belly perched above her legs.

"Preeti," Manmohan asked, "do you think I could cook the beans with the gizzards?"

"Gizzards get done in one whistle, dad."

"Yes, so they will become a little soft with three whistles. So what? I am sure the beans-gizzard combination will be good."

"Eight dad, eight."

"Ah," said Manmohan.

During lunch the gizzards were soft as baby food and the beans hard as pebbles.

"This is good, dad," Preeti said, trying not to sound sarcastic.

Manmohan beamed. "I had held your mother's hand and I had said, 'Radha, I will be both mother and father to your children'. The poor woman, how she worried about all of you."

After Preeti had eaten, Manmohan ladled some of the beans into his own bowl and took a mouthful.

"Oh," he cried, "this is terrible! We will get diarrhoea. Well, never mind, one learns through one's mistakes, no?" And he threw the concoction into the bin. "We should make *bhindi* for dinner. Mac likes *bhindi*."

Manmohan cut open a new packet of oil and poured it into a bottle.

"You know, I haven't cooked for forty years. Oh yes, forty

years ago, in the year 1960, when we were in college, me and my friends kept a stove in our room. Oh no, we were not going to wait for the mess to open; we made our own tea each morning. But since then, I have not cooked anything. But don't you think I make good *bhindi*? Cooking is easy really; one just needs to put one's heart into it. Now look at your mother, she could cook like an angel, but sometimes she was just too lazy. She'd cook anything. The thing with me is that I put my heart into whatever I am doing and I do it top-class! Preeti, *beta*, get out the *bhindi* from the fridge, will you?"

Preeti heaved herself off the futon, walked across the room, entered the kitchen and pulled out the *bhindi*. The fridge was right behind her father.

"Here, put it here," Manmohan patted the space beside him. "Or maybe," he pondered, "Maybe you should wash them. Yes, yes, wash them."

Preeti washed them.

"Your mother was an amazing woman," said Manmohan, after he had decided which onion he wanted. "I was worried about what people would say about you getting married to Mac. I am a broad-minded person but our society is narrow. One cannot disregard society. One has to live in society, and it is this society that comes to one's side when one needs help. One has to keep society happy. I was worried about the inter-caste alliance, but your mother! She looked at me and said, 'It is that boy or no one. If you don't get that boy married to Preeti then you are not a man'. Hahaha! What a woman your mother was! Do you think this is enough onion, Preeti?"

"A little more, dad."

"Yes, I think this is enough. Any more and the *bhindi* will get soggy. *Beta*, take out some green chillies, *na*."

Preeti took five chillies out of the fridge.

"Oh," said Manmohan. "That is too many. Put one back."

Preeti put one back.

"On second thoughts, maybe you are right. Take that one back."

"Dad!" exclaimed Preeti. But she took that one chilly back out of the fridge.

"O-ho! Your temper is always sitting on your nose. Why are you shouting?" and he laughed. "Remember the first time your mother saw Mac? She could not stop talking about how *beautiful* he was. Such a *beautiful* boy, she kept saying. Who calls men beautiful? Hahaha!"

Preeti wondered where this was going. He hadn't spoken of her mother with such intimacy for a while now.

"I said, 'But Radha, Preeti does not even like the boy too much. Do you see how she does not talk much about him? She might have someone else on her mind.'" Manmohan turned around and looked sneakily at his daughter. "I was right, wasn't I?"

Preeti smiled but did not answer.

"I mean, your brother was sending you all these addresses of other boys you could write to. There were too many boys. That was what I was trying to tell your mother. I was trying to tell her that there could be other prospects out there, better ones too. Hahaha! But of course, your mother's heart was set on Mac. You were looking online too, weren't you?"

"Yes," said Preeti. "It's the easiest thing to do these days. I did not write to all the boys you wanted me to contact, anyway. Some of them lived too far away and meeting them would be too much of a hassle."

"And expensive."

"Yes, that too."

"Do you think the onions are brown enough?"

"That seems about right," said Preeti.

"I will let them fry a little longer, just to draw the flavour out," he said. "Remember that evening when the three of us went out for dinner with Mac? Your mother came back and said to me, 'Did you see how comfortable they were? They are very comfortable with each other.' I put her in her place right away. I said to her, 'What do you think? Do you think our daughter is the kind who gets comfortable with strange men?' After all, you had just met Mac, no? How can you get comfortable with someone you just met? You were just being polite, but your mother, bless that woman! My God, we Indians use an awful lot of spice!" He coughed.

"Put the exhaust fan on, dad. How many times I have told you to put the exhaust on? And why is the flame so high?"

"But the *bhindi* will get all gooey if the flame is down."

"Listen to me for once, will you? Put that flame down. The baby is kicking like crazy and I hate this heat!"

Manmohan put the flame down and flew to his daughter. "Are you uncomfortable? Is the baby uncomfortable?"

"We are fine. We are fine. It's just hot."

"Yes, it is hot."

Manmohan turned back to the stove and stared into the fumes rising from the pan. "You know," he said to the fumes. "Sometimes, I feel your mother knew things that I did not. I wonder why she insisted on Mac. She would not even consider the idea that there were other boys to check out. Why did she insist so much, Preeti?"

Preeti did not answer. Manmohan turned around. He had that expression on, the one he wore when he was trying to emotionally blackmail someone.

"I don't know," Preeti said. "Maybe she just liked him."

"How did you meet Mac?"

"He was one of the boys you had sent me the email addresses for."

"But Mac is a Christian. I never sent you any Christian boy's address."

"You did, dad. Maybe because his real name is Mahesh."

"Funny, because I know I tried to keep it as close to our

community as I could. The farthest I went out was with that Brahmin boy, but he was an IAS officer. One could make an exception there."

"You sent me Mac's address, dad. You just don't remember."

"But Mac is from Philadelphia. I remember trying to find someone from Philadelphia because it would be easy for you to meet the boy, but I remember that I could not find anyone. It's funny how many things I seem to have forgotten."

Preeti said, "Let us make some potatoes too, dad. Here, let me chop some." She took three big potatoes out the fridge. "Do you think these will be enough?"

"Yes. Preeti, did you lie to me about the email addresses and the whole online bit?"

Preeti looked him straight in the eye. "No, dad."

"So, I found the boy for you?"

"Yes."

"A Christian boy?"

"You are more broad-minded than you give yourself credit for, dad."

"You were not having an affair with Mac the whole time?"

"You know I would never have an affair. Do I look like the sort of girl that has an affair?"

"No, you are a good girl."

Preeti smiled. "And you are a good dad, dad. I wouldn't do anything to hurt you. You sent me the address, maybe by accident. But it's true, you did."

Manmohan kissed his daughter on the top of her head.

"I knew you would not do anything to jeopardize the family name. You know, if people heard about you having affairs, they could turn to me and say that I raised a characterless girl. Some people even implied as much, but I said to them that Mac was Radha's choice, not yours. You would marry anyone we asked you to marry. I said it is time they too broadened their minds and looked for good boys, not just boys from within one's caste. Times have changed and one must live with the times, no?"

"Yes, dad."

"I am so proud of you!"

"I am proud of you, dad... Dad, I'm tired. I am going to sit down, okay?"

"Yes, yes, and leave the potatoes. I will fry them."

Manmohan heard his daughter shuffle into the living room. Yes, he thought, as he washed the potatoes, one must live with the times. And for some strange reason, he thought of the time he had first given Preeti a watch. She had just finished her tenth grade and had passed with good marks. The watch had been a reward. He had had the watch in his suitcase for years, before he finally gave it to her. He was still convinced that it had been an HMT with a silver strap. Yet, when Preeti returned home for the vacations, she was wearing a Titan, with a brown, leather strap.

It was funny, the way one's memory worked. Even now, after so many years, he remembered giving his daughter a silver HMT. He did not remember buying a Titan, but Radha had insisted that the watch he had given their daughter had been a Titan. "You are growing old and senile," she had said.

"Preeti," Manmohan called out suddenly. "Was it really a Titan watch I gave you, after your tenth grade exams?"

"Dad! You know you did."

"Yes, of course. It's just that I am growing old and senile."

Perhaps, the GIG is so protective of her parents' sense of honour because her parents are so protective of her – her place in society, her reputation, her future, her ability to fit in.

They wish to spare her the pain of being an outcaste and so they shower her with a hundred rules – who to love, what class or caste to love within, who to cheat, what to endure. Many a GIG learns to snuggle into the tight little corner she's been painted into, telling herself that they love her; they want her to be happy. Many, but not all.

You see, there are GIGs and there are BIGs, and then there is Padma. Most Indian girls respond to society. The good girl conforms to rules; the bad girl feels cheated and breaks the rules. But both understand how the machine works. Somehow, the machine eluded Padma. She did not understand the machine or what purpose it serves. Like a curious animal on a forest trail, she went down one path, then another and then the next one, just to see where it might lead.

You have to envy her. She was an adventurer down to her toe-nails. Like a surfer who tackles the highest waves, she took risks and waited to see if she would stay on her feet. When she fell, she didn't panic. She lay belly-up, floating in the rocky waters, and waited for something to happen to her: a rescue, a shark, a mystery island. And something always did.

Talk of the Town

Padmavati was the talk of the town even before she grew to her full height.

That her looks were so striking was one part of it. Hair that caressed and moulded itself along the curve of her buttocks and stopped inches from the backs of her knees. There was more than one soul in Jodhpur that used to stand around near Christ Church Senior School and pray to be turned into the rat's tail end of her plait. And what hips! Just like the new, white heroines on Star TV – small hips, thin legs, tight jeans, wide bones, and to crown it all, that long straight hair, more gold than brown, ragged edges tantalizingly sweeping back and forth across veiled buttocks. But that's about as much foreignness as her slender body allowed. For the rest, she was every inch the Rajput princess without an estate – which she was. A long, slightly hooked nose that screamed aristocracy; fine, arched brows; dark eyes that slanted up ever so slightly at the outer edges; skin the colour of ripening wheat; long arms and long fingers that busied themselves often twirling a strand of her hair.

However, these evident charms were not the only reason Padmavati – Padma to family and friends – became the talk of the town. Beautiful young girls are too numerous to interest more than a few onlookers. Padma's fame emanated from one long, intensely hot summer, when she was fourteen.

The unfortunate incident involved her running away with the man who drove the family car. Bapabhai came from a village that had been once ruled by her ancestors. He bowed and called her '*Bai-sa*', little princess, and had been in the service of the family since Padma was eight. When she was fourteen, she decided she wanted to marry him. He was somebody she trusted, who told her stories about an idyllic village where everybody loved everybody else, where women grind bajra on an ancient, hand-drawn chakki and buffaloes turned oil mills. He wasn't bad looking either – shining chocolate complexion, big moustache, black eyes.

Padma had decided to run away. The trouble was, Bapabhai was the only man she was allowed outside the house with, and he had control of the car. Besides, she remembered the humiliation of her last attempt well enough: she had been eight years old, and had tried to run away after school but, not knowing where to go, she had ended up hiding behind the shacks of the gola-walas who sold green and red ice golas at the school gate. They had caught her, and brought her back home, and her family had given her two sound slaps, and decided to hire Bapabhai to drive her to school and bring her back.

This time, the fourteen-year-old Padma turned to Bapabhai with a plea he was very hard put to refuse. "Marry me," she said. He was, of course, already married but that hardly mattered in these parts; her own grandfather had had three wives. So one day, she stole some money from her mother's household account drawer, stuffed her schoolbag with spare clothes and chocolates, and set forth to live in Bapabhai's village.

Three days later, she was found washing her face at the village's hand-pump, school skirt already quite filthy since there was an acute shortage of water and nobody took any more baths than was necessary. The 'wedding' hadn't happened, to her family's immense relief.

Padma too did not seem displeased to see her parents, stern-faced and harried though they were. Without any fuss, she fetched her schoolbag and meekly sat inside their car.

They packed her off to a boarding school in Jaipur the same year. She ran away from the hostel once, received stern admonishments and was warned that if it ever happened again, she would be dismissed.

She ran away again.

Word was sent to her parents and they had to bring her back home. They got her readmitted to the old school and her father began to ferry her to school himself. When the school-day ended, her mother came to pick her up, an ancient family retainer driving the car.

Things were quiet for a while. But it was too late to salvage her 'name'. Padma was already the talk of the town.

Rumours abounded. Some said she had actually married Bapabhai. Some said she was mentally unhinged, or that she was possessed by a spirit. Others said she had been sold into a brothel by Bapabhai, and was rescued after one whole week! And everyone agreed on one thing: this girl could never be married into a respectable family now. In short, Padma was treated as a closed file in the nuptials department.

Taking courage from that fact, many men would make bold remarks during lunch break when all the girls would flock to the locked gate to buy ice-gola and chana-masala. Men would call out her name, say they would marry her. Others would suggest that she could be had without being married, so why bother?

Padma had few friends, most of them of her own assiduous making, and these few would often suggest that they stop visiting the gola-walas. But Padma was unfazed. She would walk down alone, order a gola, calmly stand there while the gola-wala hurriedly packed together the ice and dunked it into a bowl of orange syrup. She would look around with unseeing eyes, an almost smile on her thin, etched lips. She would pay the gola-wala, start sucking at the gola, unhearing of any remark calling on her to suck a sweeter stick than the one in her hand. When the bell rang, she would stroll back to her class, head bent over the leaf-bowl, lips busy, shoulders hunched. Tall, slender, the colour of new wheat.

Meanwhile, Padma's parents plotted. What could be done to restore the lost lustre of a reputation without which the girl was as doomed as one who is limbless and blind? How to wrest from the mouth of a wolf-world, a decent Rajput wedding?

It would help if their own daughter was on their side. But she seemed to live on some plane they couldn't hope to understand. At school, Padma seemed to totter from one exam to the next, passing with only a slim margin. She wasn't interested in any particular kind of music. She wasn't interested in astrology, or the myths of Rajput valour. She wasn't interested in religion or yoga. She wasn't even interested in dressing up and attending weddings like other girls.

However, Padma was unusual in one thing. She rarely defied her parents. She did whatever they asked of her. If they asked her to switch off the television and sit down with her books, she did so. If they asked her to make a cup of tea, she did so. If they asked her to show some mercy for her old, harassed family, her eyes would fill up with tears. If they asked her to promise that she would never, ever repeat some unfortunate act, like running away, she would immediately promise – never again.

In her own way, they had to concede, Padma was a very good girl.

They decided to put her in a college with a hostel regime that was so strict, no girl was allowed to leave its premises at any time of day or night. The hostel was surrounded by high walls and barbed wire, and a watchman kept guard twenty-four hours, along with some ferocious-looking mongrel dogs.

Her mother spent mornings sitting near the phone, expecting to be informed by the hostel warden that her daughter had gone missing. But Padma did not run away this time. But then, she did pretty much nothing else that year. She did not study. She did not attend classes. She did not enter any talent contests. She was a visible presence on campus though: slightly hunched, sometimes barefoot, hair caressing her buttocks. Sometimes, she walked up to girls who were not from her own batch or dorm and strike up a light conversation. Sometimes, she read a romantic novel.

In her second year, Padma was told to be more participative in college. She obeyed. She volunteered to help backstage during the rehearsals for the drama club and was often seen running about with props, helping other girls with make-up, pausing occasionally to lift her honey-gold hair and twist it into a loose bun that came undone every three minutes.

The same year, Padma was caught cheating in her exams. She hadn't even bothered to construct any elaborate ruse around the act. Quite simply, she'd folded sheets of notes several times over, stuffed them into her pockets and during the exam, unfolded them and began to copy. Her getting caught was almost a certainty. The examiner had rarely seen such blatant cheating, nor such a student who did not plead to be forgiven and given another chance.

Padma instantly became the talk of the college. Her parents arrived post-haste and did all the pleading on her behalf. She was given a warning and allowed to sit for the rest of the papers. Three days later, during the next exam, Padma was caught cheating again.

She was suspended from college immediately. Her parents decided it was high time Padma found her own home. Jodhpur was impossible. So they went to a sympathetic aunt's home in Jaipur and a quick groom hunt was undertaken. Three prospective families were identified and were invited to lunch, dinner and brunch respectively.

Oh, if the town could have seen Padma that weekend, she would have been the talk of the town all over again for very different reasons.

Yellow chiffon sari, long hair loose, brushed away from her delicate face. Clear eyes, rarely raised except when she spoke. An almost-smile on her mouth. Moderately high heels in matching yellow. No trace of make-up. Nose elegantly studded with a tiny, solitary blue diamond. Left wrist bare, a simple leather-strap watch on her right wrist. Tiny pearl earrings, a gold chain with a pearl pendant on it clinging to her neck. The faintest trace of lipstick glossing her lips. Hanky clutched in a half-fist. Voice husky but soft, low. Skin like sunlight-drenched ripe wheat on a misty winter morning – fresh and crisp.

The matter was settled by dinner-time that Sunday. The lunch party had agreed and wanted a quick wedding. The dinner party wanted more time, probably to conduct inquiries in Padma's native town. They also wanted the girl to finish her BA. So her parents settled for the lunch party instead, because they seemed to be in a hurry too.

The lunch party had come all the way from Sitapur. The groom had a reasonably solid business, which he had been so busy building that he had grown to be thirty-three years old without bothering with this other business of going to lunches and dinners to look at good Rajput girls. Thirty-three, for a man, was not too old, but the family was anxious to seal the deal because it was not likely that they'd land a nineteen-year-old catch elsewhere, certainly not such a visual delight as this Padmavati, the only child of parents with significant properties in Rajasthan. They guessed too that her parents were shopping around for grooms and wanted matters settled soon. So the Sitapur party decided to propose before the girl found someone younger, richer, more eager.

Padma's parents accepted the proposal. They even suggested that instead of Jodhpur, the wedding be held in Sitapur, where they had many relatives and even co-owned a crumbling ancestral house. This was true. The house did belong to Padma's mother's widowed aunt. It was a different matter that these relatives had been neglected for over two decades because they had so little social currency. Yet, for a wedding, they would make themselves useful.

Padma really was an obedient daughter and the wedding went off more smoothly than anyone had dared hope. The few whispers circulating amongst mammas and sisters about the bride's torrid past began circulating only on the actual day of the wedding. As the mantras were chanted, they dissipated like jealous smoke from the holy fire of matrimony. The beautiful bride dazzled all eyes as she said goodbye to her parents amid a clutch of weeping, rustling women.

Her mother held her a long time in a parting embrace, while furiously whispering into her daughter's gold-encrusted ears.

"Don't do anything troublesome, do you hear? Don't run away from your new home," she said and after a pause, added, "Or from any place you are taken to live."

Racking her brains, she clutched her daughter harder to her weary bosom and rattled off a list of instructions. "Don't wear clothes that might shock this family. Don't steal from your in-laws. Don't steal from the servants either. Don't sell off your jewellery. Don't sell the furniture. Don't drink anything alcoholic without your mother-in-law's permission. Don't touch anything narcotic. Except on Holi, and even then only if your husband insists. Don't talk too much. Don't stay too silent. Don't read sexy novels. Don't watch sexy movies. Don't go out with strange men. Don't go out with familiar men either. In fact, don't go out with any man who is not your husband."

She paused to wonder whether she had covered all bases – what else could possibly go wrong? – and then she heaved a sigh of relief as Padma dutifully nodded. "Yes, Mamma."

"Promise, baby?"

"I promise, Mamma."

Padma was as good as her word. She didn't drink unless her

mother-in-law suggested it. She didn't steal. She wore nothing but sarees. She didn't run away. She didn't read anything except the newspapers, and didn't discuss politics unless her husband brought up the subject.

Three months later, Padmavati made an unmistakable pass at her husband's sister.

A professor of literary theory once had to teach us poetry. He had the eyes of a poet and a poet's slow walk so we supposed he would do all right. He did not do too badly. His theories gave a much wanted practicality to poetry, which was useful and charming. He taught twentieth-century poetry. The earlier poems, he said, were too difficult: he understood the later poems better. What he could not understand was why Sylvia Plath should have killed herself. She had it all, he said. She was educated and could work if she really wanted. She was not poor. She was not born in an oppressive society. She was, after all, an American. Besides, how could someone with children have killed herself?

Ours was a small, local college without a meaningful library and with no computer whatsoever. We could not get to wikipedia and arm ourselves with facts to bolster our arguments. All we knew was that there were men who, under exactly the same circumstances, had killed themselves. Hemmingway, we said. What about him? Hemmingway killed himself and he was educated, well-travelled, not poor. He was American and he had a child.

Hemmingway, said the professor, was a man. A man has reasons to die.

Out of Here

Hi. This is Silky again.

There is one final thing I want to say about GIGs. They are supposed to want to live.

Padma's birthday was also the anniversary of the day that Padma first tried to kill herself. Actually, not really; she didn't half-properly try. But she did take a razor to her wrist and carved two sets of angry trilateral slits. A man's safety razor, the kind they show in the ads. It is called a 'safety' razor for a reason, but even so, she had been vicious. The slits were uneven, jagged. The scars would stay a long time.

When the bandage came off, Padma let me look. Angry pink welts, with a swollen toughness enveloping them. She let me look for a few seconds, then turned my face towards her so that she could look into my eyes.

This is the most intimate moment possible between any two people. The moment of acknowledging death. The moment of telling life to go fuck itself somewhere else. This seeking of finality, of being driven over the edge by the uncertainty of tomorrow, of being impatient for tomorrows, being exhausted with the routine of inhale-exhale that passes for life – this is probably the world's commonest, best-kept secret.

Her gaze was unflinching. There was no shame, no remorse in her eyes. This would be another of those dark secrets we first kept from each other, and then told each other.

She was living with her parents again. They had moved to Delhi and worried constantly about her – what to do with her, what would become of her, what would everyone say? Everyone in that house was miserable, Padma too, and her misery was an odd thing to me. I was learning, for example, that misery does not always love company. Misery sometimes likes to be left alone, to marvel at its own absoluteness. To play with itself. To see how far it could go, without losing its grasp on itself. At least, that is how it was with Padma. She did not want me to commiserate. She only wanted to tell me the truth.

Once before, she had looked at me with such an expression. It was in college. That time when she confessed to eating up a pastry all by herself, wolfing it down quickly while I had gone to the bathroom, because she didn't want to share it. Stupid things like that would make Padma guilty.

But this time she wasn't guilty. A suicide attempt was not a treat she'd let me share. And it was a treat – an indulgence we knew we could not afford too often, for every time we hurt ourselves, we had to hide the marks. We had talked about dying for several months now. We talked about everything – love, loss, death, suicide. We talk about the desperation that led you so far, and the temptation to relinquish your hold on all desire. The fear of it. The longing for it. But it was just talk; we didn't have enough guts to test our longing. But now, finally, she had had the guts.

"I don't. If I had the guts, I'd have cut deeper," she said.

"But you did not want to."

"I did not want to," she admitted.

"Then why did you try?"

"Because I got tired of not trying it. Just talking about it – how to do it, how it could be done, how much it would hurt. I got tired of empty talk."

"You're lying, aren't you?"

She laughed. Taking her hand away from mine, she buttoned up the cuff of her long sleeves.

"I just got angry. Lost my temper."

I understood that. Padma sad was Padma safe. When she was upset, she would lock herself in her bedroom and sob to her heart's content. She never cried in front of anyone. Or she would make me come with her for long, winding walks around the park. Or we'd go somewhere and have endless cups of black coffee. Always battling the melancholy.

Melancholy had became a way of life for us and it was alright, as ways of life go. But sometimes, melancholy turned to rage. Rage against the well-kept secret of routine living, coping, laughing it off, forgetting that there's misery simmering below the surface of our skins, and breaking out in boils as we went looking for something we knew we would never find.

I knew this rage well. I knew how it strikes – beginning with discreet breakdowns at manageable intervals until suddenly, you begin to ask: why?

There wasn't any single 'why'. All our whys would roll themselves into tight balls of imploding rage and collide and collude and form one big cannon-ball of rage. And then you would begin wondering: 'Okay, why not? Yes, why not?'

This was the dangerous moment. This was the time when you could finally gather the guts and kill yourself. It would put an end to all cycles of disappointment, judgment and desire.

But Padma didn't rage like I raged. Tempestuously. Anguished and contorted and unbearably ugly in the bathroom mirror. Her rage was different. It simmered. Her pigheadedness gave it a frightening craft-like quality. When she said she lost her temper, it didn't mean a spontaneous loss of rational thought. No, it wasn't like that at all.

Her temper rose like a moon-drawn tide. It rose and rose and lashed at her nerves until she bled it out of her system. That's why

Padma angry was Padma dangerous. Anger made her cold and horribly practical.

For instance, she had carefully planned this attempt at slashing her wrists. She had taken the trouble to buy movie tickets for her family as a special treat. When the first dream-sequence song came on, she complained of a blinding headache and walked out of the hall. Then she bought a razor and went home.

I asked why she bought a new razor.

"My old one has been lying in the bathroom for eight months. I thought if I used it, I would have to get a tetanus injection," she said.

I clicked my tongue to indicate that I understood; it made perfect sense. A moment later, we both burst out laughing.

That's how we were. We laughed because we didn't want tetanus injections in case we outlived ourselves. We laughed because we wanted it to stop – the rejections, the injections, this city where we had no novelty because it was so familiar, our endless walks, our dependence on each other, and all the things we hid from each other in some strange bid for dignity.

Who knows what drove her over the edge this time? Did her father send yet another missive to her husband, begging him to take Padma away? Or did her husband show up for a weekend, only to humiliate her thoroughly? Did he sleep with her when he made these short visits, raising her parents' hope that he would forgive her and rehabilitate her as a proper wife? Or did somebody say something as she walked past – a stranger whose voice should not have carried so far?

I knew she would never tell me. Just as I knew that I could never tell her about how my beloved Papa had taken to peeking at my cell phone when he thought I was asleep, checking to see if I had been talking to boys.

Looking at the pink welts on her wrists, I was thinking that it would be easier for me because I won't have to push away my people when I do it. I already spent so many hours alone at home, locked in with my computer. Nobody looks in on me except at meal-times. I will not have to buy a few hours of solitude.

Poor Padma! She had to rush through the whole experience because she knew the movie would end soon. By the time she had bathed, cleaned up the bathroom and pulled on an over-sized hoodie, her family was back. She pretended to be aspirinned out of all ability to converse as they went chattering on about how the movie ended. She didn't cry. She just lay in bed, begging the maid to stop jabbering, or go somewhere else and shout if she must shout.

I would not do it this way. I would sit quietly on the bathroom floor, watching the blood clot. But I would panic if the bleeding did not stop. As I looked at Padma's sad eyes, I wondered whether I would have anyone to call, once the panic set in.

That evening, we were both in my house. Her father called her after some time and shouted at her for going out of the house without telling him where she was going. She quietly apologized over the phone, said she was with me and would be home in an hour, and remembered to tell her father to take his medicines on time.

After she hung up, she began to cry. She was standing upright, her back pressed against my wall. She had raised an arm to bury her face in the crook of her elbow. With one foot, she began kicking my cupboard.

I watched, not daring to touch her. There was something forbidding about her body. Like she didn't want to be touched right now. I waited for her to calm down.

When she was done, she came back to sit beside me. I took her hand then.

She said irritably, "Don't!"

"What?"

"Don't look at me like that. I know you are looking at my wrist."

And she burst into another round of sobbing. I let her put her head in my lap and stroked her hair.

Mid-sob, she suddenly stood up. My heart was in my mouth for I didn't know what she might do in this state. But she just strode across the room and switched on the fan.

"No point being hot as well as miserable," she said, sniffling.

Then she returned to the bed and buried her face in my lap, and I did not know whether she was laughing or crying.

Most people we interviewed agreed that Padma didn't fit into the GIG mould. And yet, they would probably see facets of Padma's face refracted into the mirror when they looked at themselves, or at other people in their lives.

Every family has women who refuse to be trapped by narrow definitions or rules. Somebody's mother is a chain smoker who taught her son to light his first cigarette. Somebody's grandmother drinks out of a steel tumbler – single malt, neat. Somebody's aunt ran away with a colleague after ten years of marriage, leaving behind three children to fend for themselves and an ailing father – with no explanation except a high degree of boredom. Somebody's virgin sister is on drugs. Somebody has self-inflicted scars. And somebody has slept with various men without guilt or fear for no better reason than this: she wanted to.

Baby Fat

Three years after they had hugged tight and cried buckets worth of farewell and don't-forget-to-write and I-swear, Deepti didn't want to meet Reeta, after all.

It had been three whole years since Reeta's wedding and a year since they exchanged photographs of themselves in their new avatars. In her picture, Deepti was seated at her desk in a printed silk kurta; hair swept up in a roll and held up by a wooden stick with silver *ghunghroos* on one end. Reeta sent a picture of herself with her husband, Prasad, holidaying in Montreal.

Now, she had written again, attaching some pictures of baby Preeta – a cute amalgamation of Prasad and Reeta.

Deepti had sent back a one-word email: 'Congratulations'.

She didn't want to have anything to do with Reeta – the Reeta who always had a boyfriend at all points of time, who put on a deep brown-red lipstick just to go to the corner store to buy an ice-cream, who once lived with three boys in small flat, with no other women in the house. Reeta, who had sex before she was married, without even hoping to be married to the same guy, and who returned from assorted rendezvous with stories of how far the current boyfriend went. Reeta, who wept hot tears of rage if you refused to let her borrow a new set of clothes when she had a hot date in the evening. Reeta, who never visited a city, an institution, a hotel, without a stranger on her tail, some poor fellow trying to pass on a chit with a phone number on it. Reeta, despite all this, got married to Deepti's cousin's roommate's elder brother, Prasad, barely ten weeks after he professed an active dislike for the woman.

Reeta was the creature mothers frighten their adolescent daughters with. Somebody who is used and dumped, somebody who ends up trapped in a soulless, fractured relationship because she took whatever little scrap destiny doled out to her in the end. It was the only reason a girl like Deepti tolerated a girl like Reeta.

But Reeta seemed to have shed her inconvenient past like so much baby fat. It wasn't fair, thought Deepti, and easily forgave herself for not being able to stand the excess of this happily-ever-after situation. It was supposed to be good girls who are rewarded with a decent husband and the baby with the overly cute name. Girls who fucked around were supposed to end up bitter and lonely. Reeta – even if she did manage to land a rich, good-looking guy like Prasad – was not *supposed* to be happy.

Deepti thought of the day Reeta had first had sex, slipping away from the project they were supposed be working on together. She went off to a hotel (a hotel!) and returned with stained jeans. At first, Reeta lied that she'd started chumming suddenly. But a week later, she couldn't hold it in any longer, and she told Deepti.

Deepti had to work hard to hide her shock. If it had been Preeti, or even Gaurangi or Padma, she would not have hesitated to scream. How could a girl do it? Just like that? In a hotel? Just because some guy wanted it? How could she? Howhowhowcouldshe?

But this was the post-graduate MBA crowd and they were in the mother of all metros. Most girls in Mumbai pretended to be cool about sex. The boys were so cool they didn't even brag. They just let you assume that they had so much sex, so often, it was not worth mentioning. Nobody got ruffled when sex was discussed. Some girls even had to pretend to be sexually active so they didn't feel left out of the conversation.

Deepti held her peace and asked Reeta some polite questions about the experience. Her friend was only too happy to answer:

"Yes, it felt good. Yes, it hurt but everything before was nice. Oh, I don't know; we'll probably get married."

But she didn't marry that boy. A month later, Reeta got a bouquet of flowers delivered at work. It was signed by three male names. It was appalling, Deepti thought. To have three boys chasing after you and all through the same bouquet... Oh, shame!

Nobody understood why Reeta attracted so much male attention. She was not all that hot – ordinary oval face, pale brown skin, thin lips, thick waist, short legs. What was so special about her?

It was a question Reeta herself answered. She had once tried to enlighten Deepti about what sort of things boys wanted in a girl: Okay-okay hips, not too large and not too small... Boys like an okay-okay waist. Not tiny. Not a big paunch either... Boys like big breasts.

That ought to explain it, Deepti had thought. Reeta seemed to be describing herself. Maybe it was true. Maybe it was the bright lipstick and the tight jeans. Maybe it was the sex she was willing to give, or the twinkling eyes, or the giggle. Whatever it was, she seemed to have what boys wanted, and then she found a boy she wanted and got him to marry her.

It seemed like there was no punishment for bad behavior, after all. Deepti could have cried when she saw the photos – ma, papa, baby in the pram, dappled sunlight, house, the foreign income. Oh, the injustice of it all!

She stared at her computer screen. A new email had popped up. Reeta saying: "Hey, I'm back in town. When do I get to see you? Muah Muah Muah."

Deepti groaned. She could say she was busy this week. But it wouldn't help. If not this week, the next. If not the next, the next. It was best to get it over and done with.

She wrote back: "Heyyyy! Soooo good to hear you're back. This Saturday? Coffee?"

Reeta wrote back at once. Within three minutes, in fact.

"Why just coffee? Let's go OUT!!!"

'OUT!!!' could only mean going to a pub. Deepti knew the routine. Tight black jeans, high heels, dark lipstick, and Reeta moving her head from side to side, eyes shut, chin tilted upwards as if she was just waiting to be kissed. She had accompanied her friend on one such outing before and even then she had known instinctively that Reeta behaved like this each time.

Oh well! This once they could go OUT!!! In future, she would beg off, making up some excuse. So Deepti picked a club she hated – a place with super-loud retro music and too many teeny-boppers. That takes care of conversation, she thought.

Saturday arrived. Deepti spent over an hour dressing. She chose to put on a short denim skirt on top of printed leggings, a full-sleeved top with a deep V, flats on her feet. She considered heels briefly, but sensibly decided to wear something she could drive in. Besides, the club would be too crowded and she would have to stand most of the night. She checked to see that her car had enough petrol, checked twice to see that she'd locked the door properly, and set out exactly half an hour later than she should have. She was certain that Reeta would be late.

But Reeta was already there, waiting on the pavement outside the club. High heels, skinny jeans, a stretched beaded top. Deepti recognized her, of course, but her eyes widened as she took in the woman standing out there, anxiously looking right and left. That butt was not 'okay-okay'. Its sheer size overshadowed the big breasts. The butt had clearly lost the race to her waist, which was very far from 'okay-okay', now that it hung a few inches over the top of a smart golden belt. The hair too seemed to be recuperating from a particularly savage blonde job.

Suddenly, it struck Deepti that her friend was alone. Of course, she hadn't said anything about bringing a husband along. Perhaps her husband was babysitting. But it still came as a surprise: Reeta going out alone? And looking it: Alone.

The chocolate brown lipstick was too loud. The heels looked like they hurt. The jeans looked too new, as if they had been bought especially for this evening. They seemed so stretched at the seams that one could almost hear the fabric making frantic gasping noises.

Deepti stepped forward, arms extended.

"It is good to see you," she said. And she meant it.

In our part of the world, it is enough for a man to not be an alcoholic, not to beat up his family, not to shrug off financial responsibilities. He would be considered a worthy proposition, a fitting match for the best of girls, a good husband. But for a woman, making money and being non-violent is not enough. Even chastity is not enough.

GIGdom is gauged through a complex set of parameters on an unstable graph. You could be a gentle, refined, virginal, practical, frugal, impossible kind of GIG, but your halo is sure to be dulled if your mother runs away with the cook. Or if you develop an unreasonable aversion to nice clothes and dinner parties. Or if your father commits suicide after defrauding a bank. Or if your brother gets arrested for loitering in public places at night or smoking pot. All of this will affect a GIG's marital prospects.

She is judged by the family she's born into, the number of phones she carries, the boys whose company she keeps. She is not expected to be wholly innocent in the ways of love, but she must still bear the burden of knowledge – she must be ignorant about how to go about making a career as a porn star or a pole dancer, for instance; but she must know how to read people's minds.

A Little Knowledge

Hi. My name is Ruby.

In my family, everybody talks about 'good girls' in the same breath as marriage. I learnt that goodness was equated with not going out of the house, except to school, and socializing with extended family and in-laws but not being too involved with people outside the community. A GIG is one who knows things without having to be told, one who is always ready to do what you ask of her, one who tells the truth if you want the truth but is willing to tell lies when that is in the larger family interest, one who dresses nicely but doesn't spend much money. I also learnt that spending too much time with yourself would taint you, make you a lesser GIG, just like it had tainted Seema Bhabhi.

A lot of this was picked up at my Maama's house where they live in a joint family. During one winter visit, my mother let it be known that she was on the lookout for 'a good girl'. Maami, of course, claimed that there was one, ready and waiting, right inside the house.

"She's a good girl, Mansha. What else can I say?" Maami pulled up her legs, crossed them at the ankles. She rocked back and forth for a minute and re-wrapped her shawl around herself.

Ma seemed to hesitate. A good girl isn't a piece of cake these days. Why, finding one wasn't a piece of cake even in her own day, back when you couldn't do the things that everyone seems to do now without the foundations of the house quaking in horror or the high ceilings weeping with shame. Besides, these days, everybody called everybody a good girl. What did it mean?

She leaned back and stretched her ankles, drawing the edge of the quilt over them. Maami let a moment pass.

"*Arre,* Mansha, what should I tell you? The world has changed. Nowadays, forget the daughters, even daughters-in-law cannot be counted upon to move their hands and feet. Take this one, our Seema. She's come from Ujjain. A town of culture and heritage, is it not? But what use is that? Such culture! She only eats and sleeps and sleeps and eats. *Arre,* she does not even bother to feed the household, such is her love of sleep."

Abruptly, Maami stopped talking. Seema Bhabhi stepped into the room with a tray of tea and a dish piled with hot *namak-paras* and spiced *papad,* sprinkled with onions and tomatoes chopped super-fine. She smiled at nobody in particular, swallowed the sudden silence and politely stood beside the bed for a minute.

"Tea," she said.

Seema Bhabhi tends to state the obvious.

"Thanks Bhabhi," I said. "But you are too much. Just because I said I loved *masala papad,* you didn't have to… with guests in the house and all, you're doing double hard work!"

I stole a glance at Maami. She sniffed and looked away while her hand dug into the *namak-paras.* Ma pulled at Seema's elbow. Bhabhi perched at the edge of the bed for a minute but quickly excused herself again.

"This is so delicious," I said, licking the spice off my fingers. "She must have been working all afternoon, chopping and roasting and frying this stuff."

It was as if I hadn't spoken. Maami crunched the *namak-paras,* waiting for the shadow of her daughter-in-law's hospitality to disappear before she spoke.

"All this is only for you. And you come for just two days. Most days, she sleeps right through the evening and to hell with the appetites and habits of this household."

Ma quietly sipped her tea. Her mind was whirling so hard, it made me dizzy just to be near her. She changed the subject.

"This girl… her name is Shanno?"

"Mansha, the girl is a gem. All day, morning to night, even at midnight, she stands beside me in the kitchen. She will cook and wash and scrub and will faint rather than utter one word of protest. My own daughter did not do as much. Now what more can I say, now that I have said that?"

"Her mother?"

"Does a bit of tailoring. Lives three rows down. I tell you, I saw this girl when she was this high, and decided to take her under my wing. So yes, she is poor. But what does poverty matter, Mansha? It is better to be poor, I tell you. What do you think, our prima donna comes from a royal palace? *Arre*, you see her house in Ujjain. It is not even their own. Something rented. Rented! That's after living in the same place for sixty years. *Arre*, if it was not for these damned tenancy laws, these people would have been out on the street. What more can I say, now that I have said that?"

Ma complained, "Your cups are too small. Tea is done in one gulp. Aren't there any big mugs in this house?"

I knew my cues. Ma couldn't ask for tea just five minutes after we had been served. I was expected to make my way to the kitchen now. I would look around helplessly until Shanno asked what I wanted. I would say that I am going to make another round of tea. Shanno wouldn't let me, of course. As guests, we didn't lift a finger in the kitchen. Shanno would make more tea. I would hang about for a few seconds making protesting noises before giving up, leaning against the wall. After a bit, Shanno would say I shouldn't stand out in the cold, why didn't I just go downstairs? She'd bring the tea. So I went through the charade.

Ma, in the meantime, would ask questions which she thought

unmarried girls like me should not hear. Questions like where did Shanno sleep? Where was her father? What prevented him from making a noise about a daughter spending nights outside? Was her mother with some new man? Was Shanno illegitimate?

When I returned to the room, Maami was answering these questions in an offended tone.

"*Arre,* Mansha, what do you think? She is not a servant. She is like my daughter. I do not give her a salary to spend time in the kitchen. I give her protection, and anything she needs. Her clothes, her expenses, I take care of her just like my own child."

Ma was anxious that the match be pulled off but she didn't want to sound too eager. Our driver was thirty years old and, as far as we knew, unattached. Unless he had a childhood wife hidden away in some village. At any rate, he had not brought a woman to the city yet. But the problem was that we were giving him a room to live in. My brothers said we'd lose him in a year or two if we didn't make a move towards rooting him deeper into our household. There was space on top of the garage, so we were getting a room constructed. But it is common knowledge that the moment a man living in a city has a room of his own, he brings a woman into it. Ma decided that the only way to prevent undesirable women from entering the fringes of our household was to acquire a desirable one. Ma wanted a girl who was used to hard work, someone who made herself useful and could not quit so easily. The driver needed a bride. We needed two extra hands in the kitchen. It was a perfect plan.

I was not much help in the kitchen. Ma took a certain ambiguous pride in my helplessness on the domestic front. She liked to sigh, particularly in the presence of extended family members, how Ruby has been brought up like a princess, the only girl sandwiched between three brothers, God knows how her baby would ever manage? Ma would then moan about what the world might be saying about my household skills.

Actually, the world didn't say anything – partly because it didn't see much of me and partly because whatever it thinks, the world rarely communicates directly. It likes to whisper instead. At any rate, whatever I could or couldn't do, it was taken for granted that I was a good girl since I spent so much time at home, with books.

Towards Shanno, unfortunately, the world aimed no benevolent gaze. It assumed the worst. Her mother was a single woman who claimed to be a widow but who could say for sure? The young daughter worked in Maami's house, and the world (and my mother too) wondered what to think, considering there are two young sons in the house, not to mention constant comings and goings of guests who had young sons of their own… Well, what more could be said now that this much has been said?

A confirmation of the goodness of Shanno's character was in order and Maami was giving it her best shot.

"Mansha, I swear, I have shielded this girl's reputation like you shield your Ruby. She sleeps with me, eats with me. I tell you, I am giving you a girl who is like my daughter. What more do you want me to say?"

Ma turned to me.

"The tea is coming," I said. "Shanno said she would make it."

"And you too listen carefully," Maami went on, her face growing stern. "I will not hand over this girl to a man who cannot feed her and clothe her. I know her temperament. If she doesn't get nice clothes, the kind we wear ourselves, she will not be happy. And who wants a young girl's misery on their conscience?"

"Bhabhi!" Ma said. "You know well enough food is not a problem by the grace of God. What we eat, our driver eats too, and so will she."

"I suppose she might," Maami said. "And this man?"

"*Arre,* he is a good boy. He's been with us ten years, just like this Shanno has been with you. And I trust him fully. He is like a brother to my own girl here."

This was a blatant lie. The driver had been with us only five years, and did not live with us yet. I did not even know the name of his village.

"Thirty?" Maami frowned. "This girl is not more than seventeen."

"*Vaise* he must be closer to twenty-eight," Ma said quickly. "These people don't keep birth records, you know. I just gave you a round figure. Better to judge a bit more rather than a bit less. But you know as well as I do, it is not a good idea to match a girl with a boy of her own age. A girl is only as good as the hand holding hers is strong."

Maami clicked her tongue in assent. My mother forged ahead.

"What is ten years between a man and a woman? There are nine years between you and my brother. There are eight years between me and my mister. Now look at my eldest. He married one who is only a year younger, and ... what shall I tell you?"

The bone of contention between my eldest brother's wife and my mother was that the young wife would not wake up early in the morning to make tea. Instead, it was he who woke up first and made her a cup. Maami clicked her tongue in sympathy.

Ma complained, "A girl must have respect for her husband. Otherwise, what is there to say? I tell you, ten years or even twelve years' difference is fine. A good girl is made better by knowing how to respect her elders. Let her begin with her own husband."

The door creaked. Shanno slipped into the room, tray in hand. Ma immediately blessed her and under Maami's watchful half-smile, took the tray from her hands. Then she asked the girl to sit beside her. Shanno, wisely, did not. Instead, she drew up a small stool.

"This girl is such a good girl. Much better behaved than mine," Ma said and chucked Shanno under the chin. Shanno blushed with pleasure and gratitude, hands folded in her lap, but she said nothing.

Maami sniffed. "Let us hope she stays that way."

Girls are never praised to their face, not by the women who

bring them up. I knew this theory and its practice well: to praise your own girl for being good was like praising yourself, and to let a girl know that she was beautiful or talented was to ensure her downfall.

There was no such restraint on other people's mothers, though, especially when they are trying to woo you away for a potential groom.

"Why won't she?" Ma gushed on. "She is such a good girl that I feel like stealing her away from you. And such a pleasant face too! What do you say, Shanno? Shall I take you away?"

Shanno smiled and looked at Maami, who sent her away with the empty plates and cups. It only took a glance.

Maami leaned closer to my mother and whispered.

"Don't think she doesn't know what we are talking about. This girl is smart. She understands things even if you don't spell it out. She was asking me just yesterday, 'Why does Ruby's mother keep saying I am such a good girl?' She knows what happens next."

Ma laughed. "What do you expect? Is there a girl so good in this world who does not know who wants what, and who is praising her for what reason? Such a girl is called an idiot, not a good girl."

A little knowledge, it is said, is a dangerous thing. But in our culture, the tiniest scrap of knowledge must be distilled and tempered and made innocent on its passage through to the young girl's mind.

For instance, it is good to know your bra size. It is not so good to know where to buy a shocking range of underwear or sex toys. It is good to know you will be married some day. It is not so good to know the thereafter. It is good to know how to set up a kitchen. It is not so good to know how to negotiate with rough brokers and tough landlords on your own.

Overseas

Hi. This is Preeti again. I am one of those who left. Crossed the seven seas so I could become someone else. You have to go somewhere else to be someone else.

Why does a girl want to live alone? I wonder too. Why leave? Why go away? Why face all the hardships? It is not expected of us. If we were to say we don't want education in distant lands, that we don't want distance, or even an education, these things would not be forced on us. Girls are not boys.

Boys are coerced into being successful professionals. Girls only have to do well enough at school and maybe college. And any school, any college is as good as another. Yet girls go away. Some take the bus to a school ten stops away, some move to another town, some move to large cities, some to a different country. And when they come back something has changed. People look at them and say, "Oh there she is, she who does not stay at home, who knows how to live by herself."

There is, despite their attempts at modesty (most girls come home to neat salwar-kurtas and soft tones of speech) a boldness to such girls. Those who have left their hometowns for large cities know how to pay their bills, look for new accommodations, apply for cell phones, ride overcrowded public transportations and, in emergencies, take taxis to their apartments at midnight. They know how to survive in a man's world, and it is agreed that women cannot survive the man's world without the help of men. These girls, those who have left their home-towns know how to ask men for help. They know men.

I left home too. For years I was the successful student every parent wants their daughter to be. I did well. I did tremendously well. I stood first in class. I topped my university. Soon I was the youngest person teaching at the Masters level – modern poetry and applied criticism. Of course, I was not a professor or even a lecturer. I had no designation. For a proper designation I would need a doctorate and our university did not offer one. And if it had, I would not have pursued a PhD at my university. I was suddenly ready to leave town.

My parents, though anxious, stood aside and let me apply for scholarships. I had been a good student and any opposition from my parents would mean they were thwarting my future. Papa gave in reluctantly, and when I received the best scholarship that was to be had, he could not stop boasting. Ma looked at me wistfully. She kissed me on my head and she kissed my palms. She told me she would miss me but she was happy.

I was not just going away to another town, to another bigger city. I was going to America. Every time I thought of the journey I trembled. I saw before me an adventure, a narrow opening bursting into a glittering newness. I lay sleepless at night, my heart unable to contain the images that rose before me – I am going to be free, I thought. Free!

I shivered with delight. I pictured my feet strapped in thin leather sandals, my calves bare, a soft cream-coloured dress blowing against my knees. I thought of sand and of long empty streets and the night alive with peace. I pictured myself walking everywhere without the fear of being harassed and teased and labeled. And yes, amidst all of that I pictured love, unconstrained by rules. I thought I would abandon all aims.

My teachers were happy for me. I deserved it and I would, they were sure, make them proud. I would do remarkably well in an

American university. It was believed that cracking the American education system was like shelling peanuts. An average student in India could excel in America and I was so above average. God alone knew what I was capable of.

Only Ma, with her new wistfulness, did not tell me I would excel in America. Ma and, strangely, Yogesh-sir.

Let me tell you about Yogesh-sir. He is a shy person. He has a sweet smile and his pale lips always look a little bruised, like he has just returned from a brisk walk on a cold morning. His eyes are quiet and small but when he smiles they light up – still shyly. He is the shyest person I know and I suppose when I first fell a little in love with him it was his awkwardness that attracted me most. He was out on a quest for clarity and beauty and he was, despite his misty eyes, the most insightful teacher on the campus. Nothing was complex. Nietzsche, Kant and Saussure resonated in his heart with pure simplicity. He taught me that that there could be nothing truer than suffering, more honest than pain, more desired than death. He taught me that all knowledge, indeed, anything that was anything, was a tool to pass time meanwhile. Life, he said, was nothing but a meanwhile.

His eyes were liquid with existentialism, his sentences heavy with poetry. I and my friends would go to him after classes and ask if he could please explain what another teacher had made impossible to comprehend. Could he please paraphrase whatever in god's name Kamal-sir was trying to say? Could he please, please take some extra classes and finish up somebody else's syllabus. He did. He always could.

Sometimes, after everybody else left, I lingered on and asked for more clarifications. And once, when he accidentally brushed my hands, I wanted to cry. And once, months later, when he held my hand, I removed it immediately and was very disturbed. And then, once, when he asked if I would marry him, I said I would ask Papa.

Papa did not agree. Yogesh-sir and I were not of the same community. He was also very poor. He had no real estate. He lived in a rented house which he shared with his younger brother. He could not decorate me with gold. He could not take me out to fancy malls. His parents lived far away in a hilly village and he had left his hills to come to this city so he could get an education. No, he was no match for me. Had I gotten an education so I could live in poverty with a man who was not even from our community?

I did not fight with Papa. I had by then learnt to love simply for the sake of loving. Or perhaps, I had by then learnt never to love too much. Or perhaps I was a coward. Either way, I did not fight Papa. Instead, I went to Yogesh-sir and let him know that Papa had not agreed, that Papa did not even want to see him, that it was all decided. Then I started to cry.

I surprised him by crying and he surprised me by not protesting. He shrugged and said, "Oh well," and we sat with each other for another half hour not knowing what else to say.

For months, we avoided one another. If we crossed paths we smiled politely. I wondered if his heart beat a little faster when he saw me the way mine did when I saw him.

Then he went home to his hills, to his parents who were so proud of him. He went for two weeks and when he returned, he brought a wife along. And just like that, quite suddenly, I felt free of him. When we saw each other again, my smile was not polite. I teased him and called him *chhupa rustam* and we were friends again. The awkwardness was gone and so was my love. He was now my friend. I even thought of his wife as my friend. I was now free and could go around with my endless scholarship forms.

His marriage had established his pragmatic nature. He was not romantically inclined after all, despite his soft eyes and sighs and his talk of death and elation through nihilism. We started to hang out together once again. We drank tea and ate breakfast before classes. I asked after his wife, he asked about my plans. I was honest with him, he tried to be secretive – wife, family, these are private matters, after all. But secrecy came hard to him and I always teased him after his failed attempts at sophistication.

Then I got my scholarship and became a small-time celebrity. Congratulations and good-wishes. I stood amidst all of this and was overwhelmed. It is true that one does not know what one has until one leaves it all behind. And yet, I was eager to leave, to be away from all the people who knew me, to live a life defined by my own rules.

A week before my flight, Yogesh-sir asked if I would join him for breakfast in the canteen. I can see myself now, sitting across Yogesh-sir, the two of us dipping our parathas in bowls of yogurt. I was ecstatic and slightly scornful of him – his simplicity, his sudden marriage to a stranger. I was full of cocky abandon and I wanted to laugh at him. I was so happy that morning. I remember that it was bright but I don't remember if it was warm or cold. I don't remember what either of us wore but I remember feeling snug. I did not know then that I would forever remain fond of him.

Then he asked me why I was going away. "Why are you going?" he asked.

I shrugged. I did not know how to answer him. I could not tell him, like I could tell others, that I was going to get my PhD, to make money, to get a career. He would know that it was not entirely true. Finally, I told him I was going to do all the things I had never done.

He did not ask me what these things were. Instead, he put his food down and looked at me quietly.

"You walk with such a swagger," he said, and I smiled. "In the old days, they forbade travel overseas. They said the sea corrupted the soul, made it impure. Nowadays, when we have given up ships, the wind corrupts us faster."

I laughed and took another bite of my paratha. I wondered if he expected an apology from me.

"You know," he said. "Sex is not like in the books. It will not make you happy. It will not mend anything. It is rather difficult and sometimes if you are not in love, humiliating."

That is when I looked up from my plate. I saw that he had planned his sentences and he had come here to warn me against what lay ahead, and to tell me what lay within him. I felt bad because I had no clue that marriage was so difficult for him. I wanted to comfort him but I was no longer in a position to do that.

I wanted to contradict him too. I wanted to tell him I was talking about being able to pay electricity bills and buying cell phones, but I did not. It would not have been entirely true.

Nothing had actually happened between me and Yogesh-sir, but in a way, something had happened. I was always conscious of him. I compared my new American teachers to him. I thanked him mentally when certain lessons, too difficult for my *firang* peers, were easy for me. If I saw a green motorcycle, I thought of him. And in the middle of a date, I would suddenly think of Yogesh-sir, of his caution against lovelessness.

I did not write to him to say that sex was sometimes freedom, it was sometimes difficult and sometimes it was not, and sometimes it was just that – sex and nothing more. I did not write to say that I had not settled down with anyone else yet, because I could not marry him. I did not write to say that if he had put up a fight for me, I would have put up a fight for him. Had he not left me alone to untangle all my mess by myself, we would have been together, untangling it together, bit by bit. I did not write to say that I was, at the moment, actively looking for love and I was sure I would find it and then sex would become what it is like in books. In the meanwhile, I was enjoying the overseas.

Things change. Generation to generation, state to state, notions of GIGdom vary.

Some Indian communities don't bat an eye when young people have pre-marital sex. They never have cared. Girls can afford to get pregnant, or get divorced, and yet not worry about finding love and security later. Boys can fall in love without worrying about being beaten up by the girl's brothers.

In much of India, both boys and girls work hard at making a living and helping the whole community survive. In some communities, women – nearly all women – smoke. And drink. And swear. They use terrible swear words and sing songs loaded with sexual content and innuendo.

There are hundreds of communities in the subcontinent and not all of them place the same value on innocence, sexual or social. But they lie on the fringes of our cultural consciousness. When people talk about the typical 'bhartiya naari', *the image that pops into our heads is that of a sari-clad woman with long hair, someone demure and skilled at housework. We do not think of a tobacco-chewing field labourer with muscles on her arms and a song on her lips. Both are equally Indian, of course, and who can say who is the better woman?*

Yet, there is no denying the fact that the latter is rarely upheld as a model for the rest of us to emulate. Perhaps, because the latter is too poor and too busy to be serving as a role model.

Even so, things have changed. The women who were sari-clad (complete with pallu over the head and sindoor in the parting of their hair) have daughters who live alone and are answerable to no-one for their conduct.

These daughters do not always have to leave the country to transform into another person. Sometimes, they just move to a bigger town. They might be refused accommodation simply because they are girls wanting to live alone (it has happened to us). They might be asked to pay up extra money for the privilege of a landlord who does not poke his nose into your business. They might have their refrigerators inspected by disapproving cooks who judge their morals based on how much dinner was consumed and how much wasted.

These daughters might hide their lives from their mothers, afraid of being judged too severely. But to their own friends, they are still firmly within the GIG brackets.

And yet, many a GIG has spent a lifetime worrying about the past catching up with her; worrying that she will be found out as a fraud – a woman who did not deserve the blessings of a stable relationship.

And as many women cling to an insane hope that perhaps, one day, the past will come back to knock at her door, pay her a social visit, speculate casually about what might have been.

Gifts

The *baraat* was late. Nobody complained because such was the nature of *baraats*. They arrived late, in a burst of deafening noise that woke up half the city, with the groom looking either insufferably smug or comically piteous.

The bride, despite the long hours of waiting in her room with her many friends and aunties, would usually look radiant. Reeta was no exception. However, she was very glad her parents-in-law had insisted on having the wedding at the Taj. She had spent five hours in five-star comfort, where the air-conditioning could be attuned to her nervous temperature. She felt warm at first with seven kilos worth of *ghaagra,* a one-kilo tissue dupatta and what seemed like half a ton of make-up. Now, she was suddenly feeling cold.

Mary sat next to her, squeezing her hand. The other girls had rushed out to welcome the *baraat*. There would be some good-natured exchange of curses, as was customary, at the entrance. The priest had resumed chanting with a bit more enthusiasm. The guests finally sent up a little prayer of thanksgiving because now, dinner would be served, after all. The patient hotel staff had pulled their smiles out of whatever dark cellar smiles slid into over the course of a typical Indian wedding. The fairy lights seemed to twinkle again.

After that, everything was a blur. Reeta's mother burst into her room to say: "*Chal*."

Mary scrambled up, unwrapped a new set of gold *jootis* with tiny pink stones scattered over the toes, placed them on the floor. The bride stepped into them with a tremulous sigh. Mary then gathered up the flowing, seven-kilo fabric off the floor, and held it to one side so Reeta wouldn't trip. They began to walk.

The next thing Reeta remembered was the stinging in her eyes because of the *havan* fire, the smell of ghee and her mother's hands adjusting the veil around her head every thirty seconds. She knew Prasad was sitting beside her, and although she had gone as far with him as possible and though everyone else knew that this was a love marriage – his extended family hadn't finished muttering under their breaths that she had seduced their *seedha-saada* southie boy, this northie witch – she did not dare raise her eyes to his. She had been strictly instructed not to look up until after the ceremony.

She did sneak one look during the *var-mala* exchange – he looked so different with that tilting turban and the tent of flowers framing his face. She wanted to giggle but wisely pressed her lips together and bit her tongue hard simultaneously. It was her trusty giggle-suppressing mechanism.

Then suddenly it was over. Her mother was wiping her eyes, her father was standing, misty-eyed, with an empty basket of rose petals. Mary rushed up, along with two other aunties and they ushered her back into her own room. Another mad scramble followed. They removed her tissue dupatta, dusted the extra *sindoor* off her hair and forehead, retouched her make-up, added a few flashier, fake jewels to her head and hands – "for the photo session" – and draped her head with a brighter dupatta with a solid, half-kilo gold lace border. This time they left her face unveiled.

Meanwhile, Prasad waited on a dais mounted with two oversized chairs with silver arms and legs and deep red upholstery. Here, the newlyweds would sit, standing up each time a guest approached to congratulate them, touching the feet of the elders and cooing to the kids, accepting gifts, bobbing their heads to numerous *namastes*. All the while, flashbulbs would be going off, and they would pose endlessly, grin endlessly and fight the temptation to snap at somebody.

But before Reeta could step out and brace herself for the umpteen dives she'd have to make for the hundreds of pairs of feet, she happened to glance up and there he was, almost blocking her way: Shailendra.

She knew his face in a fraction of a second though it had been almost seven years since she'd seen him last, and despite the fact that he had been a smooth-chinned adolescent back then. Shailendra Jain, from Hyderabad, Banjara Hills.

Her family had moved to Hyderabad for two years, and they had stayed in a new apartment block in Banjara Hills. He lived right across. He was in Class XI, Commerce. She was in Class XII, Arts. He had already found out her name: Reeta.

They were the same age but he was a year behind because his parents had made him drop a year, after his tenth board exam results; they wanted him to take the exam again to improve his scores and take up science with maths and then do his engineering. He took the exam again and improved his overall score by 0.63 per cent, and eventually his parents resigned themselves to the idea of a BMS-MBA son instead of an Engineer-MBA son.

While he may not have been focused on organic chemistry or calculus, Shailendra Jain of Banjara Hills, was very focused on what he did want, which was that new girl, the one with liquid coal eyes and significant bosom. Shyness was never one of his failings, so he lingered at his gate until the auto-rickshaw that dropped her off from school every day, chugged up. As soon as she stepped off, he went up and said: "Reeta! Hi!'

Reeta was so taken aback at this bold display of familiarity that she stood there, just looking at him for a few seconds. He did look vaguely familiar, but he was certainly not from her section. How did he know her name? Even if they were in the same school, this was a bit much. Nobody just came up to a girl, not where she came from, and certainly not good boys who lived in the colony. If anybody saw and told his parents… but perhaps his parents didn't mind. This was Hyderabad, after all, not Allahabad.

But her own parents were very much from Allahabad and it would never do to be seen standing around with a boy. She tossed back her plaits and went into her building.

Shailendra didn't take this rude response too much to heart. Girls were like that, it was universally known. It was too much to expect a girl from a good family to just start talking to him the first time he spoke to her. So he went on to establish his credentials and intentions in the simplest way possible. He formed a routine.

Every day after school, he waited at the gate until her rickshaw arrived and she stepped off, then he nodded, said hello and waited. She invariably glared, tossed her plaits and went off. But each day, the glare seemed less sure of itself, and on the sixth day, Shailendra took heart from the way it seemed be more a rising and falling gaze than a glare. He went out and bought a greeting card from Archies.

It said 'friendship' in silver, curvy letters on the outside, atop a soft-focus picture of two toddlers (male and female) sitting side by side, barefoot, on a park bench. On the inside, there was a whole list of things 'friendship' was supposed to mean. 'Friendship means never having to say sorry or thank you' etcetera. He spent a whole evening trying to say something clever that expressed his personal sentiments too. He tried out several drafts on scraps of paper but nothing seemed appropriate. Finally, he settled on: "Dear Reeta, Hi! Will you be my friend? Many regards, Shailendra."

The next day, he held out the card in its pale pink envelope. Reeta stared at it as if it contained some fatal vermin or a bomb. She didn't take it.

Shailendra fell into this new routine in his plodding optimistic way. He presented the card to her again, the next day, and undaunted by her refusal, yet again. On the fourth day, Reeta rather dramatically stopped, glared harder than usual, snatched the card from his hand and – eyes steadily locked onto his – tore up the card into four pieces, tossed them to the ground, tossed her hair and marched off.

Shailendra stood there, staring at the pieces. He bent, picked them up and went home. The next day, he bought another greeting card, exactly the same type, wrote in it again, and presented it to her again. She tore it up again.

And so he bought a third card and repeated the routine. This time he added another line at the bottom. "PS: I know what you must be thinking, that it is not proper to be seen giving and taking cards like this, but I only want to be your friend."

He stood at the gate, wondering whether he should say 'Hi' first or extend the card first this time, and suddenly the rickshaw was there. She was peering out, cautiously, and when she spotted him, she hesitated for a moment. On an impulse, Shailendra walked up to her rickshaw, placed the card on her lap and walked away without even turning around to see if she had ripped it into four pieces.

But she didn't. This time Reeta took the card home. She read it quietly, placed it between the folds of a history book.

The next day, Shailendra waited as usual. He said, "Hi Reeta."

Reeta had paused then, and while she did not say anything, she did not glare or toss her plaits. So it stayed for the rest of the year. Soon she was on study leave, and then she was giving her final board exams and then, she was in college. He was still in school and that was that.

Only once, they met again. He finally finished school and his father allowed him to take out the car for a celebratory picnic. That afternoon, he took the car and parked it some distance from her college. Reeta walked past. He stepped out quickly, called her name.

She stopped, she smiled.

"I finished school. My results are out," he said.

"Oh? Good," Reeta replied. "Are you satisfied?"

He shrugged. "I would have been satisfied to just pass. It is my father who has to be satisfied."

"Is he satisfied?"

"I don't know. He's not shouting at me."

Reeta laughed. Funny, the way he was talking to her. As if they talked often. As if they had done this before – stopped on the street to catch up at the end of a term.

"So, now?" she asked.

"I'm off for a picnic with some friends. Why don't you come along?"

She shook her head. "I can't."

He nodded. He hadn't expected her to come along.

"So, what are your subjects in college?"

"History, sociology, political science."

"Nice combo."

"Everybody takes it."

There was an awkward pause.

"Listen, why don't we sit in my car and talk?" he said.

Reeta looked at the car. She looked at him. She looked at the street, people walking past, standing at corners, glancing at them curiously.

"No thanks. This is okay."

"You'll get tired standing."

"I don't intend to stand around that long," she said, laughing.

He laughed too.

"Is college fun?"

"Yes."

"But it is a girls' college, isn't it?"

"Girls colleges are fun."

"Really? Well, I guess I'd have a lot of fun too if I was in a girls' college."

It was a lame joke. Reeta had heard several boys attempt it

before. And they all wore the same sort of lazy, pseudo-cocky smile this guy wore. She rolled her eyes.

"You wish." But she let him have a smile.

He tried again. "We could just sit inside the car instead of standing on the road."

Reeta met his eyes very suddenly before he'd had a chance to step away from what he'd been suggesting. She held his gaze.

"No," she said, finally.

And she didn't see him again. Until now, on her wedding day.

There he stood, almost barring her way. Reeta's heart almost stopped. It wasn't that he was more attractive. In fact, he had put on weight and lost a bit of hair. She didn't even remember his old face clearly. But Reeta's mind was darkening with a hundred insane possibilities. Why was he here? Would he try to tell Prasad that this bride was actually his childhood sweetheart, or worse, some sort of adolescent harlot? Would he create a ruckus? Would he get drunk, try to make the childish greeting card incident to be something bigger than it was? Had he found out about other men? Was he here to disgrace her? Who invited him?

Shailendra Jain was leaning forward, almost as if bowing to her. He was whispering.

"Where was the hurry? I was waiting, you know. I never forgot you."

Mary overheard. She took in this new angle, this new man, his stricken voice. She noted Reeta's hard swallowing, her suddenly cold hands. Protectively, she slipped an arm around her friend and smiled tightly at this stranger.

"Excuse me, I'm sorry but I don't think we've met," she said, and firmly steered the bride towards the silver-legged chairs.

On the dais, Reeta whispered, "Mary, he's not my–"

"Whatever. Forget it. Doesn't matter."

"What if he tries something funny? I don't even know why he's come, all the way from Hyderabad?"

"Ignore. Ignore."

He came up to the stage, along with another boy she didn't recognize. They were both carrying a gift – it was a huge thing and must have needed a dozen sheets of wrapping paper to go around it. Reeta glared at it suspiciously. It was almost as large as a coffin and almost as high as a bed. What could it be? What sort of wedding gift was that anyway? Did he get it all the way from Hyderabad?

Mary stepped up quickly and accepted the gift on behalf of the bride. She got other family members to push it behind the dias while Reeta reluctantly introduced her husband to Shailendra.

Surreptitiously, Mary tore away a corner of the wrapping. There was plain newspaper wrapping underneath. She tore away a little more and poked a finger through. Wood, definitely. But what was in the wood? She tore away a whole side of the wrapping paper as a barrage of guests mounted the dias, posed for photos with the young couple, quickly stepped away to make room for the next family. Reeta smiled brilliantly each time the flash popped.

Mary came to stand beside the bride and squeezed her arm.

"What's in it?" Reeta whispered.

"A chest of drawers. A cabinet, sort of. It's beautiful. Hand carved. Has your initials on it. And it is full of flowers. Each drawer has a different bunch of flowers inside."

"Get rid of it," Reeta hissed.

"It's beautiful."

"Just get rid of it. Ask my mom to put it in the storeroom or something. Throw it, sell it. Whatever."

"But why?"

"Idiot! He's given me a massive gift, it's probably expensive. I hope it isn't a family heirloom or something... What will *he* think?" Reeta jerked her head delicately towards the groom. "If I say now that this guy was never close to me, Prasad will never believe me."

"What's wrong with an expensive wedding gift from a friend?"

"Friend? *You're* my best friend, Mary. What have you given me?"

"Nothing. But I will get you some nice –"

"Oh Mary! Get rid of it. Please. Men don't understand if you get expensive gifts from other men. And all those bloody flowers in the drawers. Romantic dumbo... Just get rid of it."

So Mary took the gift home herself. It still had Reeta's initials on it, so she told everyone that it was a cast-off from among Reeta's pre-marital possessions – stuff that was given away to cousins and friends when a bride moved to her new home.

Mary really loved that cabinet. She loved its smooth, dark finish. She loved that its edges were rounded so that if you did bump into it, you wouldn't hurt yourself. She loved that it was low but not too low, that it was squat and heavy – it suggested stolidity with style. It was a perfect gift from a lover, or even an ex-boyfriend who had never quite stopped liking you.

She lined the shelves with newspaper and dried neem leaves. It was just perfect to store party tops and lingerie and socks. But then, it struck her that her clothes were personal items and she might establish an intimacy with a gift meant for another woman. So she started to use it as a book-cum-DVD store instead.

Besides, each time Reeta came to visit, she would insist on seeing the chest of drawers. She would even bring along books and DVDs to put in it, and would run her fingers over the initials.

Reeta hardly talked about Prasad. Often, she talked about how rushed her wedding was, how everything was a whirl and she didn't even know what was going on. Then a few weeks later, she admitted that Shailendra was calling, telling her it wasn't too late; it was never too late. She asked Mary if there was any harm in meeting over a coffee – surely her husband wasn't such a bully or a wimp to feel threatened by a coffee with an old friend?

Mary did not know what to say. So she said nothing. She watched as Reeta came to visit with small bunches of flowers, placing them on that chest of drawers: a fresh one each visit. She watched as her friend stood leaning against the gift, running her fingers along the edge.

And then one day, Mary decided enough was enough. She had the chest of drawers delivered to Reeta's house. That is, to Prasad's house. It was still as good as new, still full of flowers, but there was one small change. Next to Reeta's initials, her husband's initials were now freshly engraved. On top, Mary stuck a card wishing them a long and happy married life. "Belated wedding present," she said.

When Reeta saw it, she burst into tears. Prasad smiled indulgently as she exclaimed at how beautiful it was, but how Mary shouldn't have, really, and how this was too beautiful to use, right darling?

But Prasad said it was too beautiful *not* to use, and Mary would be so upset if she found out that her gift was lying unused. In fact, he began to use it for his own things – socks, underwear, ties, cuff-links, documents.

Within a year, Prasad won a research position that he'd applied for. It took him to the USA but they couldn't afford to take much luggage. So they sold some and gave away the rest. As for the chest of drawers, Reeta insisted it would break her heart if she had to part with this one thing. So they decided to hand it back to Mary, to be kept until they returned to India.

It is not impossible to follow the rules that define the average GIG. It doesn't kill you not to have fun. It doesn't even kill you not to fall in love with anyone except your husband.

What makes it impossible is to do it all with a smile. A girl who only suffers the burden of her fate is seen as a lesser GIG. The truest, best GIG is the one who likes being a GIG. She likes not breaking rules. She enjoys fitting in with her in-laws. She doesn't fret about the pleasures she is denying herself. It is nearly impossible to find fault with her. And if you are not such a creature yourself, then it becomes impossible to live with one who is.

Happy Girls

The trouble with her marriage, Seema decided, was her sister-in-law's utter, inescapable happiness.

It was possible to put up a show of tolerance, even affection for her in-laws until Sushila entered the picture as a brimmy-eyed bride crossing the threshold of a stranger. Ever since, family life had turned into a nightmare.

It took a while for Seema to understand that it wasn't about caste and it wasn't about her pre-marital involvement with Vijay. It wasn't about her own years of whining when she came into the house as a bride. It wasn't the weight or the hair – Sushila too was quickly piling on the pounds – or the wild, inexplicable fights she had with Vijay sometimes. It was just the simple fact of her sister-in-law's happiness.

It was an arranged match. Sushila met Vinay (her 'to-be' as she sometimes *still* called him), only thrice before the wedding: twice under the benign but sharp eye of her grandmother, and then once alone, in a café, with her younger sister sitting at another table. But it took her only one week to blossom into something similar to the outrageously expensive sari she wore for the wedding reception – pink dusted with gold. That's what Sushila looked like. Pink and golden.

There had been no expensive saris at Seema's wedding. It was a quiet affair at an Arya Samaj temple. Nobody's eyes shone. Nobody fed a grand dinner to hundreds of people. Of course, there was always too much money in the house and Seema could complain of nothing. She had slowly persuaded herself that there was nothing to complain about.

But suddenly, she had to contend with Sushila's eyes – first thing in the morning, lined with perfect sweeps of jet black *kaajal* – and Sushila's giggles last thing at night. A year after the wedding, Sushila still shone with health and happiness.

In contrast, there was Seema, elder *bahu*, the one who fought and wept and loved to distraction Vijay, the older brother. She was feeling grey and sadly wanting for approval.

Approval had been hard to come by right from the start because of their different castes. But at least, they all spoke Hindi. The familiarity of her tongue, her willingness to clean and cook, her non-confrontational silence had slowly eroded the in-laws' disapproval. Slowly, she began to feel at home. When she had her first baby, the household sort of sighed, as if saying: "Oh well, so she's ours now."

It was time to settle in, enjoy the baby, look forward to small joys that, her mother had dully informed Seema, did indeed exist within a marriage. But barring her complicated passion for Vijay – whom she still thought of more as a steady boyfriend than a husband – joy kept a cautious distance. The house felt cramped although it had four bedrooms and, thanks to the Jodhpur quarries owned by her father-in-law, it was opulently furnished – marble floors, marble sinks, marble tubs, marble statues, marble shelves, marble mini-mandir and marble gods. There was no reason to miss her crumbling bunglow in Ujjain. But she missed it, and how!

Here, there was no corner in which she could sit and read quietly. Here, nobody called her by her pet name: it was always the formal 'Seema'. Even Vijay had stopped calling her Simmi. With pregnancy, the extra weight arrived and firmly stayed on, despite her frantic walking in the local park. This walking about in sneakers and track pants was also disapproved of. When she began to lose her luxuriant hair after the delivery, she lost a whole lot. She lost so much hair that she cut it short, so it reached just below her ear-lobes. This won her more disapproval. It seemed that anything she did would only win resentment in this household.

On Sunday mornings, she would sleep later than usual. If Vijay was in a mellow mood, she would let him kiss her awake. She would quietly get a cup of tea for both of them, sneak in the newspapers, weekend editions and all, and go back to bed so she could listen to the morning rising and falling around her like the sated breath of a man-eater.

In contrast, on Sunday mornings, Sushila would be sitting outside, on the steps leading to the verandah. Vinay would be sitting one step above her, encircling her body with his knees, oiling her long, curly hair. As he massaged her scalp vigorously, Sushila would pretend to squeal, and then they would both laugh, oblivious to the neighbours and the elders in the house.

Seema would watch from her window. She would remember how much Vijay had loved her hair when it hung down to her waist, straight and soft as silk. Right there, her morning was ruined.

At any rate, Seema had never been a morning person. The first year after her wedding, she had struggled to wake at 6.30 in the morning, fumbling groggily in an unfamiliar kitchen, hoping to win over her in-laws. But once Shanno started to spend nights in the house, she offered to take over. Seema gratefully gave up bed-tea duty. By the time Shanno left to get married to Mansha Bua's driver, Sushila had stepped in – clinking her bangles, chirping even at 6am.

How, she wondered, could Sushila managed to be so blindingly bright and cheerful? How did she manage to giggle coyly at this stranger she had married? How had they become so comfortable? Seema herself had struggled for months to establish a degree of comfort around Vijay, for whose sake she had fought both her clan and his. She couldn't decide small things like whether she should ask him what he wanted to wear, or just lay a set of clean, ironed clothes on the bed every morning. She had not even been able to tell her husband what she wanted from him in bed. He was the one who asked her, and he continued to ask. She loved him for it, for she had never wholly lost her shyness. What mud was Sushila made of – this sister-in-law of hers who ceased to be awkward around her bridegroom from the very first night?

And how did Sushila manage to be so enthusiastic about what colours she'd wear and who she might meet in the neighbourhood? When silence loomed over the dining table, how did she manage to look at all their faces in turn as if the heaviness in the air was simply a deep contentment?

As the family basked in her sister-in-law's sunshine, Seema tried to step out of the shadows herself. Dipping into secret reserves of pride, she shook off her natural lethargy and tried to give the family everything they wanted, everything she guessed they wanted, and some things she knew they would never admit to wanting. She anticipated her mother-in-law's endless food cravings and cracked vile Punjabi jokes with her brother-in-law Vinay until his belly shook with silent, embarrassed laughter. She stopped complaining altogether.

It didn't help.

Sushila's joy was overwhelming and effortless. She didn't mind getting fat. With a cheerful sort of innocence, she went about eating and cooking and making constant demands for this or that kind of food. She liked standing around in the garden, letting the gardener do all the work. She had no desire to get her own hands dirty. She never fought for a bit of 'me' time.

She liked having her hair oiled. She liked her mother-in-law asking her to run shopping errands. If she minded her father-in-law speaking to her like she was six years old, she didn't show it. She claimed she really liked the gaudy cushion covers and the velvet curtains. She laughed out loud, on an average, every twelve minutes. Seema had once counted the number of times she had heard that burly, uninhibited laugh between 6am and 11pm and divided it by the number of minutes. It was truly frightening.

A few months later, Seema gave up. She had tended the household plants herself. She liked the warm, mid-morning solitude of the garden. But she stopped watering the plants after Sushila started to stand beside her, just for 'giving company' as she put it. She gave up wearing gold jewellery. She switched back to wearing jeans and loose cotton tops, giving away to Shanno most of the glitzy salwar-kurtas her in-laws had bestowed upon her. She just gave up.

She pretended she hadn't heard when her mother-in-law, rocking back and forth on a hard chair, complained to visiting relatives about how they had gotten stuck with an elder *bahu* who had no money, no beauty, no skills, and who was no comfort to her own ageing bones. Why could her son not have found a good Indian girl at least, even if he couldn't find anyone within the caste?

Seema reserved her smiles, saving them up for visiting relatives for whom she prepared their favourite dishes. The rest of the time, she stayed in her bedroom. After Vijay left for work, she would lock the door and switch off the lights. Her mother-in-law thought she was sleeping, but she wasn't. In the dim light filtering in from the window, she read books.

In the evening, she reserved her fragile energy for Vijay who, for all his multiplying worries of land and marble mines and his father's health, had never stopped smiling in the privacy of their bedroom. She noticed though that a peculiar sourness suffused his face when he was sitting with the rest of the family. When he looked at his younger brother's wife, he would smile a twisty-lipped smiled as if there was a core of reluctance guarding his approval of the match.

Now, when Vijay came to her at night, she would touch his lips with all the gentleness she could summon. And later, in the fractured joy swimming in his eyes, she held down and drowned all the small, wholesome pleasures that had forever scuttled out of her reach.

Seema and Vijay. It is a difficult business and how can it be otherwise? It is a love story, after all. All love stories are full of Himalayan obstacles and inevitable tragedy. There are plotting rivals, poisoned chalices, herculean tasks such as cutting a river through a mountain or creating a lake in a desert. There is war, thirst, fatal mistakes borne of blinding jealousy, when there is nothing else, you can always count on disease, decay and impatience.

Seema's love story is not the soothing, welcoming kind where you end up meeting someone who is a suitable match, and slowly grow to love this person who shares his home with you. As we have seen with Sushila and Vinay, love is unpredictable. It can strike you even if you play safe and trust parents to find suitable partners, love be damned. You would just do your damnedest to make it work. But who could foretell that a neat arrangement would translate into a series of Kodak moments – young, contented Indian couple blossoming into the kind of lovers everybody wants to see? And who could have warned Seema that her defiant, passionate affair might subside into a petty squabble for peace and privacy in Vijay's house?

It takes a lot to make a love story stay that way – a love story. It needs a woman's heart to grow a metallic sheath around her love, something that keeps ugly memories and disappointments from corroding her precious emotion. And it takes a good, patient man to kiss the unhappy woman's small demons into submission. It takes a man who can wait for her mood to turn like the face of the sky, one who can watch over her, and can stand being rebuffed by her, even though he has fought the whole world to install her in his home. It takes a man who can gather her up into his heart – every inch of her awkward flesh and every last drop of her blood – and is not afraid of the stains this will leave.

Stains

"Poor baby," thought Vijay, and wondered once more why Seema was so shy, even with him, even when they had been bound in blood, with a baby and two unhappy sets of parents to show for the absoluteness of their bond.

He had to remind himself so often that she was a shy person. Very shy. It was shyness that made things awkward between his wife and his own family, for she was too shy to immediately start gossiping and laughing with the in-laws with the sort of intimacy that only came to her with long familiarity. What other people thought was coldness was just a shyness she had been unable to shake off. Not even in bed. Always too shy to say anything, try anything.

"And when something like this happens, she just turns into a tightly wound coil," he thought. Refusing to talk about what was going on. As if her silence could melt away the truth. "She's got to tell me, of course. If she won't tell me outright, she'll say it at night."

And he knew she would not say it of her own accord. If he tried to touch her, she would say something like 'it's not the right time'; or 'my stomach hurts'. Almost as if she was afraid of her husband knowing what was happening within her body. Or ashamed of it. As if she had done something wrong.

Vijay had noticed the way she slowed down near the sofa every time she walked past it. Such a *tamasha* that night – moving the old sofa from the outer verandah into their bedroom, her doing it alone, refusing his help. He kept saying, "It's okay, baby; it doesn't show that much. And nobody knows what kind of stain it is. Seema, look, it has already faded to a kind of yellow. Like *daal* or *mehndi* or something. I mean, it could easily be *aloo-mattar* dropped on the sofa Seema!"

She had protested that a stain was a stain and she didn't want a stained sofa out on the verandah, no matter what the origin of the stain. But he knew, and she knew too, that she'd never have moved the sofa if it had been an *aloo-mattar* stain.

Vijay looked at the sofa and thought that the stain was almost decorative – like a yellow rose. It was a pale yellow, tottering on the edge of burnt orange, but leaning towards white at the centre. If you could crush such a rose into a rough green palm, that's what the stain would look like.

Vijay remembered how his cousin, Ruby, had come home crying once, after she had stained her skirt. Maybe girls just were this way. All Indian girls perhaps.

She must have been in class eight or nine at that time. Ruby had been staying with them that year, because Phoopa-sahab had got transferred to a small town where there were no good schools. Vijay remembered how word had gotten about. Even the senior boys in school had talked about the event. She must have started bleeding in the morning. She'd been sitting on her chair through the school-day and she wouldn't come over to say hello to Vijay and Vinay during lunch, as she usually did. During the maths period, some students later told them, the teacher asked Ruby a question and she didn't answer. She sat there, head bowed. The teacher asked her to stand up, and she wouldn't stand up. Three times the teacher asked her to stand and then Ruby burst into tears. The teacher got very worried. Was she sick? He asked if something was wrong. Ruby sat there, tears falling on her hands, head bowed. Another girl, a friend of Ruby's, must have understood for she told the teacher to let her be, to let Ruby go home.

Vijay remembered how upset his mother had been, the way Ruby had returned, crying all the way home.

"It must have been awful for her," Vijay thought. It had been a Saturday and the students in this school wore white uniforms on Saturday. White skirts, white socks, white shoes. It would have been better during the week because the girls wore maroon skirts. Winters were better too. Though the boys could always tell which girl was bleeding and had stained her uniform. She would be shivering with cold but she'd have her sweater tied round her waist. Seema would have been one of those girls, once, he thought. Hiding evidence of her womanhood.

Once, only once, had Seema allowed Vijay to touch her during the time when she bled. Vijay had read in a magazine that it was actually better during that time. He had asked if they could try it. She had agreed, but she didn't relax even a little. The sheets kept swimming through her head. Once it was over, she got down to the washing of the sheets immediately. He could see her even now – squatting in the bathroom, scrubbing hard at the pink-brown sheets with the hard plastic brush, in the middle of the night.

Vijay remembered touching the stain when it was fresh. It was strange. It didn't feel fresh. He didn't know what he expected it to feel like. Perhaps, rusty or red. It was just a small streak. A brownish smear, the sort left behind when mosquitoes have been biting you in your sleep, and you thwack them and kill them, and there's no evidence except the crushed smear on the sheets the next morning. Somehow, Vijay had always associated the brown streak of blood on the sheets with mornings. Seeing it at night, fresh, was strange.

Seema had just asked her husband to get her a pack of sanitary towels; she had run out and it was an emergency. He had got it from the nearest chemist shop, wrapped in a black plastic bag. Vijay had tossed the plastic bag on the sofa as soon as he entered the room. It landed near that faded yellow stain, he remembered, and he had thrown himself on the sofa too. Whenever he was sitting on that sofa, his hands would find that old stain, running over and over its outline. He saw his wife watch him, her eyes taking in the stain, his hands, the black plastic bag.

Seema reached over to pick up the bag, unwrapped the pack which was covered in another brown paper bag. She tore at one corner of the plastic pack, and pulled out one. Vijay noticed that the actual thing was covered in yet another layer of paper – bright magenta. "They've started selling them in such bright colours," he noted. "Pity there's so much plastic and paper packaging of the stuff. They could just sell each napkin as it was packed; the colours are so pretty."

Seema did not reply. She looked mildly embarrassed and turned to the cupboard to bring out a towel and a fresh pair of panties. Her underwear was kept out of sight, stuffed at the back of the bottom shelf, behind a stack of towels. Vijay sighed. When she had gone into the bathroom, he picked up the packet she had just torn open.

Magenta was a nice colour, he thought. Or is this what they called fuschia? He remembered that the ones in her drawer last month were a rich purple. "They ought to do a whole rainbow line of these. Maybe all the colours in one single pack. Scarlet reds and chocolate browns and baby blues and midnight blues too," he said to himself. It might be a cheery experience.

When his wife returned, she had changed into her night clothes. Vijay too changed and came to bed. Seema was already lying down, her body stiff. She lay flat on her back, her legs out straight and arms crossed on her middle. It was a scary pose, thought Vijay, as if she was dead and laid out for a final goodbye.

He tried to put an arm around her and when she did not move at all, he threw a leg over her and began to breathe slowly.

When she thought her husband was asleep, Seema leaned in and very softly kissed his lips. There was chocolate on her breath. Vijay kept his eyes shut and stayed very still.